Catherine of Liverpool
Parts 1, 2 & 3

By Kathleen Boyle

ISBN: 9781731136671

Disclaimer

This is a work of fiction. Names, characters, places and incidents either are products of
the author's imagination or are used fictitiously. Any resemblance to actual events or
locales or persons, living or dead, is entirely coincidental.

Cover image: www.goodfreephotos.com

E: kathdodd@aol.com

About the author

Kathleen Boyle (nee Dodd), was born in Liverpool, where she spent her childhood years before leaving to train as a teacher in Hull in 1972. Kathleen has worked as a teacher in Hull, Leeds, London and Carlisle, and at international schools in Colombia, Bahrain, Cairo, Vietnam and presently Armenia. She has written stories and poems throughout her life, and published a collection of poems about growing up in 1950s Liverpool entitled, *Sugar Butties and Mersey Memoirs*, as well as a collection of poems for children about a teddy bear called Harry Pennington in 2008. During her time in Bahrain she wrote *The Pearl House*, a short story which spans the cultural divides of Liverpool and Bahrain. The story, together with her poems, *Bahrain* and *Umm Al Hassam* were published in *My Beautiful Bahrain* and *More of My Beautiful Bahrain.* Kathleen has written a series of children's stories for Beirut publishers Dar El Fikr, two of which, *The Jewel of the Deep* and *The Magic Pearl and Dilmun*, have now been illustrated and published. Kathleen has also contributed to the Collections of Poetry and Prose anthologies; *Love, Travel, Lonely* and *Happy.* In 2015, while teaching in Cairo, Kathleen published her novella, *Catherine of Liverpool* and, during her years in Vietnam, began a revision and Part 2 of the story. A mother of three and grandmother of two, she is now into her fifth decade as a teacher, combining her love of writing, painting and travel with teaching. She is currently the Head of C.I.S. Armenia Primary School in Yerevan.

Dedicated to my children
Rory, Fionuala and Liam

With love

PART 1

Chapter 1

The Man Behind the Desk

Catherine shivered as they crossed the threshold, and pulled her shawl tightly around her shoulders. The boys were fooling around as usual, noisy and annoying.

'Stop it!' She pleaded.

Her younger brother Billy, paused briefly, breathless and bright eyed after racing Alfie up the street. He was gleefully unaware of the situation and, after a quick glance around the sparse, cold hallway, kicked his little brother Alfie up the backside and resumed their play fight.

'Stop it Billy! Can't you see what's happening?'

She felt helpless, as usual, when her brothers behaved this way. Auntie Lizzie, forlornly draped in a long, loose fitting black coat, looked resigned, and resolute; but Catherine hoped for a change of heart. If the boys would stop their silly behaviour, Auntie Lizzie might turn around and they could all go home.

To be fair, Billy and Alfie had not been told what was to happen that day. Catherine knew though. Twelve years of age, and the oldest of the children, she had grown up quickly; mothering the boys through years of turmoil.

Aunt Lizzie perched nervously on the single wooden bench, worn and splintered, like the lives of those to whom it lent support. Catherine battled her feelings of hatred towards the tired woman, whose grey, mournful eyes reflected the destitution faced by so many of Liverpool's struggling poor, for in the fading, pretty features of Aunt Lizzie, she could perceive her own mother.

In her thoughts she would often unravel the string of

circumstances which had led them to this place, and return in her mind to Great Newton St, where their home had been when Mam was alive. The kitchen stove blazing, daddy reading in his armchair and mammy busy baking at the sturdy wooden table, centrepiece of many a family gathering, were vivid fragments of her memories of home. There was warmth in the past, many smiles and a lot of love, but no matter how many times she unravelled, nothing changed and now as the man behind the dark oaken desk peered down at her, his long yellow face extracted the warmth and chilled her soul. She feared this man and more than anything she feared what lay beyond the doors separating this room from the rest of the Liverpool workhouse.

LIVERPOOL 1880

Chapter 2

Alfie Arrives

The Cattells moved to their house on Great Newton St a few weeks before Alfie's birth, and it was a rush to get everything ready. Ann Marie's sister Lizzie and her husband Denis lived a few doors away, and were a great help since her husband John worked long hours as a printer for the *Liverpool Echo*.

Catherine spent hours entertaining Billy while her mother scrubbed the house, and Auntie Lizzie called round often with hot soup and freshly baked bread. One such day they were busy together in the kitchen polishing the brasses and folding the starched white sheets and pillow cases which had been through the wash the day before.

'Well the house is starting to look lovely Ann Marie, you've done a great job,' Lizzie pronounced, hanging a shiny brass engraving of a ship at sea, above the fireplace and stepping back to check her handiwork.

'I couldn't have managed without your help Liz, and thank God it's ready to bring the baby into,' Ann Marie smiled.

'Yes and our Maude can't stop talking about having Catherine to play with, they're so close in age, like us Ann. They'll be the best of friends.'

Ann Marie glanced at Lizzie, trying hard not to laugh at her sister's remark and remembering the fierce quarrels they had over the slightest thing when they were younger. *The best of friends*, was not the term she would have chosen to describe their relationship, but times had changed and although she could still be irritated by Lizzie's fussy ways, they were closer than ever now, and she agreed that Maude and Catherine were destined to be as close as sisters.

~

The two-storey terraced house, with its polished parlour and large well-scrubbed kitchen, felt pleasantly welcoming to the steady flow of visitors, as Ann Marie and John awaited the birth of their third child. They had moved from a forlorn house near the docks, which had accommodated a family in each of its eight rooms; noisy and filthy, with a shared lavatory in the back yard and one water tap for the whole street. But John had a steady job and worked hard to save enough to rent a house of their own. It was here this cold November evening that Ann Marie put the children to bed and sent John to fetch the midwife.

Jenny Steel lived just round the corner. A robust, efficient woman, who had delivered most of the children in the neighbourhood, as well as many of their parents. She arrived with her black bag and a cheerful smile. Ann Marie's father, Callum and stepmother Margaret, had called round from their house on Peach St and stayed to wait with John. Lizzie and Denis joined the group in the parlour as Ann Marie's cries alerted the neighbours to the imminent birth.

And so it was that Alfred Alfonse was born into the heart of a city, which would be his home for almost ninety years, and into the heart of a family for whom there would be no lasting peace.

'You have a beautiful boy John!' Jenny announced. 'But I have some concern for Ann Marie. I think you should bring the doctor.'

'I'll come with you,' Cullum offered, bringing John, now in shock, to his senses, and the two men rushed out to the cold, gas-lit November night.

Ann Marie was Callum's daughter from his marriage to Fay, his Irish darling who died soon after giving birth to her. He had come to Liverpool from Killarney with Lizzie and Ann Marie to escape the ravages of the Irish famine and find work. As she grew, Ann Marie came to resemble her mother, and though Callum married Margaret when Ann Marie was four years old, he would never forget Fay, and in his youngest daughter he saw a striking resemblance; with her pale blue eyes and chestnut curls.

John had also suffered the loss of his first wife in Knowle, his home town, a fact he had kept to himself since arriving in Liverpool eight years earlier. But as he knocked at the door of the doctor's house on Abercrombie Square, long buried memories surfaced and the prospect of another lost love was unbearable.

Dr. Clegg emerged from the bedroom, having examined Ann Marie while the family sat subdued around the kitchen table, and Catherine and Billy slept soundly upstairs, blissfully unaware of the drama.

'You can go in now John. She'll pull through.'

He smiled gently and pushed his half-moon spectacles up the bridge of his nose, while John hugged him and the tension evaporated.

Ann Marie cradled the baby, as John moved close to her. She was exhausted, but he could see there was enough spirit left to bring her back to them.

'Look at our fine boy John. He's the image of you,' she whispered, full of pride.

John took the slumbering child and held him close. 'Dear God Ann Marie! I thought I'd lost you.'

'Well you thought wrong didn't you? Do you honestly think I'd leave you all? I've a little lad needs a mammy, as well as his brother and sister, and I've a husband needs a wife. I'm going nowhere!'

By Christmas, Ann Marie was well enough to walk out with her family, and one crisp, blue-skied morning, trees bare-branched and starkly black against the winter sun, John proudly pushed the pram, while Catherine and Billy clutched their mother's hands as they made their way to Peach St to visit their grandparents.

The walk took them along Brownlow Hill, past the workhouse, a towering monster of a building which stood as a bleak warning to those who were audacious enough to fall upon hard times. Inevitably, they glimpsed a few of the inmates.

'Not a pick of flesh on them,' Ann Marie whispered, disturbed at the sight of two little girls forlornly lingering in a gated yard. 'It's a terrible place to end up, especially at Christmas.'

'Their only crime is poverty,' said John.

The girls at the gate watched as the family passed by, and Catherine tightened the grip on her mother's hand. Their presence seemed to threaten her safety and she wanted to pass that place quickly and rid her mind of the image, although it would remain and resurface in the bleakness of her future.

LIVERPOOL 1888

Chapter 3

The Door Closes

As Catherine stood beside Auntie Lizzie, her fear was extreme.

Lizzie, small and frail, quietly waited her turn in the draughty room, watching the line of feeble people as they whispered their plight to the grim faced man. She was weary and not sure she had the strength to do what she had come to do. Who would want to? Who would want to commit three little ones to the workhouse?

She had agonized for weeks before today, but it had to be done. Money was short and it was a struggle to feed her own children, let alone three extra. And yet these were Ann Marie's babies, and her heart was breaking. She gripped Catherine's hand. Her gentle niece stood silent, pale as lilies.

The poker-thin man beckoned them and, with startling efficiency, inscribed their names in a book almost as big as Alfie. Auntie Lizzie signed the book, and they were lead away. Bereft, she watched the children go and not a night would pass without Catherine creeping into her dreams with the fearful eyes that Lizzie saw before the door closed.

Catherine Cattell   age 12
William Cattell   age 10
Alfred Alfonse Cattell   age 8

LIVERPOOL 1886

Chapter 4

Dreams and Secrets

Catherine loved to spend time with her brothers at the Pier Head, watching the massive liners, brim full of people, glide away from the harbour, carrying thousands of hopefuls to their promised land.

'One day I'll do that.' Billy would say, with such certainty that no-one ever doubted him. Like many a Liverpool boy, he was fascinated by the mystery surrounding the ships and curious to know the places they had been. While Billy dreamed of boarding a ship and sailing away, Catherine longed to sweep the sky, like the seagulls. She envied the ease with which they would glide and dip to catch the fish churned up by the motion of the vessels as they navigated the River Mersey.

Lately the children had been spending more and more time at the Pier Head and, although she was only ten, Catherine was wise enough to sense that all was not well at home. Billy and Alfie were content to be sent off with a penny each and big sister to look out for them, but Catherine was worried. The happy home life they once enjoyed was no more, and she wished she could tell Maude her fears, but they were too deep to find a voice.

As her Aunt Lizzie had predicted, she and Maude had become best friends and with only a year between them, they enjoyed playing together, skipping up and down Great Newton St, as horse drawn carriages bumped along the cobbled road.

The girls were as different as you could imagine. Maude had long dark curls, rosy cheeks and brown eyes, in contrast to her cousin's grey-blue eyes and fare complexion. Catherine felt safe with her cousin who was always full of ideas for games to play, and she had not wanted her worries to encroach upon the happy times they spent together.

One day she tripped and fell in the street, grazing her knee.

'Come on Cathy. Let's get you home.' Maude had said, oozing sympathy.

'I'll take myself.' Catherine had insisted, distraught.

'I'll come with you and tell your mam what happened.'

'No, Maudie. I'll go myself!'

She shrugged off her cousin's helping hand and limped home alone. Looking back at Maude as she reached the steps of her house, she felt guilty for treating her that way, but could not allow her to see what had become of home, and her mother would not have wanted her to bring anyone in. She had lived like this for weeks now, hiding the secret, trying to be normal.

Chapter 5

Irish Melodies

Ann Marie had been ill for some time.

'She looks like a ghost!' Margaret had told Callum as they lay in bed one damp October night. It had been raining all day and the wind was rattling the windows. Little pools of water formed on window ledges as the misery outside began to encroach on their living space.

'It's been a while since I was there and no sign of a visit from them, so I thought I'd call in. I couldn't believe my eyes when she opened the door Callum, she's so thin and very pale, not herself, that's for sure.' Margaret confided.

'How long's she been that way?' Callum responded, drowsily.

'Lord knows! She acted like all was well; said she felt fine, just a bit tired, and told me to stop fussing. "You're ill," I said, "and you've to see a doctor!"'

'And will she?' Callum asked, alarmed at the news.

'She said not. Said she's just tired, as any mother with three young children would be.' Margaret snuffed the oil lamp and settled under the blankets.

'What did John have to say?' Callum queried.

'That's another thing. There was no sign of John. I said I was going to have words with him and Ann Marie says she hardly sees him!' Margaret lay still, watching the dancing shadows of tree branches on the ceiling as she recalled the encounter with poor Ann Marie.

'Doesn't sound like John.' Fear stirred in Callum's gut.

'I know love, but Ann Marie said the children haven't seen him for weeks. He leaves first light and comes home when they're asleep in their beds.' She placed a comforting arm around her husband, suspecting unwanted change on the horizon, which would adversely touch the lives of all concerned.

'I'll go round first thing, Mag.'

Callum had very little sleep that night and was at Ann Marie's door early next day. Bright autumn leaves splashed colour on the grey cobbled roads and the air was fresh and clean after the rain, but Callum's senses were aware only of his daughter's plight. When she opened the door he could see that his precious girl was gravely ill.

'Hello daddy.'

She knew his heart would break to see her like this, and so it did. Callum could hardly stop himself crying out with shock at his daughter's condition. How could John allow this to happen? Why had her father not been told?

He took his daughter in his arms and carried her to the doctor's house. Ann Marie hadn't the strength to struggle.

'Will you do something for her?' he pleaded.

Doctor Clegg, irritated by the early morning intrusion, softened at the sight of the young woman before him. It was obvious to both men that Ann Marie was dying. The consumption had reached its final stages.

'I would say it's a matter of weeks Callum. Take her home and make her comfortable. I'll be round with something to ease the pain.'

As the fragile flicker of Ann Marie's life ebbed away, John sought comfort in drink. Consumption had taken his first wife. He knew the signs and could not bear to watch her fall victim to its ravages. He stopped going home, spending hours in bars, unable to accept the truth of his situation. Catherine did whatever she could to elicit his help, albeit a child's cry for help.

'Come home dad.' She would plead as he left for work. 'Mammy needs you.'

'I'll be home Cathy, but it'll be late. You look after your brothers now.'

The door would close, leaving his child in the cold hallway, afraid.

She had not known fear before now, secure within her family and trusting her mother and father to provide all she needed, but everything was changing. More and more she was left to care for the boys. She washed clothes, lit the fire and made soup every day. She tried to discipline the boys but they ignored her and ran wild most of the time.

'You're not our mammy!' Billy would say, as he continued his endless tormenting of Alfie, who was usually happy to join in, but often came off worse when his big brother got too rough.

'Leave him alone, Billy! He's smaller than you and you should stop when he tells you to,' Catherine would cry.

Billy was a live wire, never still and boundlessly energetic. Maude's dark curls and robust complexion were mirrored in his features, while Alfie shared Catherine's fair skin and delicate frame.

Sometimes, when John was out late, Catherine would climb into bed and lay beside her mother, holding her soft hand as she listened to the laboured breathing of the sick woman. She wanted to stay close, and hoped that soon her mother would get better and daddy come home again for tea and she would dance for him by the fireside, the way she did when everything was perfect.

One night she fell asleep beside her mother and was not disturbed by John's arrival. He had spent the whole night away from them. Catherine and her brothers scoured the streets searching for him. They asked around the local pubs and his place of work, but they discovered he had not been there for weeks.

It was the next day that Grandma Margaret called to the house and found Ann Marie so ill. The day after that, their granddad took her to the doctors. When he brought their mammy home he carried her to bed and there she remained.

The children stopped searching for their father and stayed home. Other family members arrived at the house. Auntie Lizzie, Grandma and Granddad stayed through the night and people they had never seen before who had travelled from Ireland with Callum came to the house. They sat around Ann Marie's bed remembering good times and softly singing Irish melodies.

A priest arrived to give her the Last Rites, and it was as if the house she had so carefully tended held its breath, waiting for the moment Ann Marie would breathe her last.

Catherine was allowed to be a child again. The adults took responsibility and she spent time with Maude, who did her best to comfort her as they sat on the front steps of the house, too sad for play.

'I wish daddy was here.'

'I know.' said Maude. 'Your mammy needs him.'

'We all need him,' Catherine murmured, scanning the busy street for her father; but the autumn mist, which had descended on the city, offered no hope, as barefoot children dodged carriages passing to and from London Rd, and grim-faced adults, engrossed in the weaving of their own intricate webs, went about their day, oblivious to the sadness, as Catherine and Maude held hands and waited.

Ann Marie died early on a Sunday morning as damp trees shed the last of their bright leaves. The family gathered to be with her as she passed, and witnessed her last breath as, in despair, she spoke the name of her beloved.

'John.'

KNOWLE 1888

Chapter 6

A Family Divided

Mary bustled around the shop arranging freshly baked, warm bread and spiced buns ready for opening time in five minutes. Her shop was the most popular bakers in the area, and Mary prided herself the best window display in the town.

Jimmy, her grandson, had just finished the night-shift, leaving the store room packed with enough bread, cakes and pastries for the day. The queue was already forming outside as early shoppers arrived to claim the freshest goods. Saturday was the big day for fancy cakes, which would grace the table at Sunday tea-time, and the colourful display looked a treat. Before long Kate, Mary's daughter, would arrive to help behind the counter but, as Mary raised the window blind that morning, she was unprepared for what she saw. Through the green, mottled glass appeared the distorted face of her son John.

Mary gave him a much needed motherly hug, although she sensed his return was not a joyful one. No words were spoken except to establish that John needed sleep. Mary sent him upstairs to the apprentice quarters, where there was a bed, and carried on the business of the day, wondering all the while, what dreadful events had brought him home in this sad state.

LIVERPOOL 1888

As the door closed, Catherine watched Aunt Lizzie's tired, grey countenance, hoping even then for a change of heart. They had reached the other side and were now workhouse inmates.

'William and Alfred Cattell, follow me.'

A young girl stood in the shadows, not much older than Catherine, but wizened and haggard beyond her years. The boys were quiet now.

The girl set off along the dark corridor which tapered into the distance like the throat of a huge monster. Sensing Alfie's fear Catherine held his hand.

'C'mon Alfie. You'll be alright; I'm here to look after you,' Catherine whispered.

The girl stopped and turned abruptly. 'No, not you. You 'ave to wait.'

Catherine felt her throat tighten. 'Wait for what?'

'Someone else'll fetch you. You'll be in the women's block.' The girl's abruptness provided no comfort for Catherine, whose devastation was now complete.

'But these are my little brothers! I 'ave to stay with them. I look after them. My mammy said I 'ave to.'

'Sorry luv, boys and girls separate. C'mon yous two,' The heartless girl sneered.

Alfie's hand tightened around Catherine's. 'Not without Cathy,' he wailed.

'Listen to me lad!' the girl bullied, poking Alfie's chest. 'Yer in the workhouse now an' whether you like it or not, you an' yer sister say goodbye now!'

Terror gripped Catherine as the thin rope of a girl, forced Alfie from her and dragged him along the dismal corridor howling, while Billy struggled to break free. Two older women emerged from a door at the end of the corridor and engulfed the children, leaving Catherine alone.

~

Lizzie went home and wept until her eyes swelled.

'What's the point Lizzie?'

Her husband Denis had been prepared for this, but he was a practical man and saw no good come of fretting over things that can't be helped.

'You weren't there Den. You didn't see their faces as I walked away. Poor Cathy'll be all alone in there. She'll never forgive me. Poor, lovely Cathy.'

'There was no other way Liz! I couldn't see my own children starve and my wife destroyed. We've done our best Lizzie. Your father's ill and your mother needs rest. Since Ann Marie died everything's all fallen apart. The children are better off there; they'll be fed and clothed. That's an end to it Lizzie. Now look to your own children.'

Lizzie wiped her eyes. She knew he was right, but that didn't make it any easier. The only solution would be for John to return safely and do his duty, but after two years the likelihood of that happening seemed remote.

LIVERPOOL 1889

Chapter 7

The Choir

Seagulls swooped beneath the slate grey sky, stark, white wings captured by a stray sunbeam. Alfie watched them fly above the workhouse and knew they were bound for the Pier Head, taking his thoughts with them. He tried to picture the scene that had once been so familiar; white sails, webs of ropes and pulleys, ships with curious names that Catherine would read to him; *The Spice Queen, The Dawn Rose, The Molly Baggins*. The three would play at spotting boats and just as the swallows would fly away for winter and return in the early spring, so the boats would come and go with surprising regularity. Billy would always know when one was due back and worry if it was late.

'The sea can be like a terrible monster,' he would say to Alfie, as they lay in bed. 'It can gobble you up and take you to its dark, deep depths. Never to be seen again.'

Alfie would lie awake, afraid the sea would find him. But Billie wasn't disturbed by such possibilities, and would sleep soundly dreaming about his future life on the waves.

Alfie had lost his boisterous, mischievous ways. The workhouse routine allowed no time for play and life had become a serious affair. For days he had been unable to eat. He thought about Catherine, worried and lonely.

Days passed and wearied him. He and Billy had tried to find a way to see Catherine, but the rules of separation were strict and virtually impossible to penetrate. One night in a fitful sleep he saw his mother, beside him on the bed, as he remembered her when she was well. She waved to him and smiled gently, so vivid he thought he might touch her and reached out his hand, but she faded and he awoke in the cold, hard bed, but he recalled the dream the next day and smiled at the memory as he swept the workshop floor.

From time to time the choirmaster would scour the workhouse for children who might be included in the choir and during one of these scourings, it was discovered Alfie had a good singing voice. Consequently he was enlisted and from then on, his life changed for the better. The workhouse choirboys had special treatment; they were frequently on show to visitors and needed to look clean and healthy. It would never do for one of the little 'angels' to collapse from starvation.

That he could sing had come as a surprise to Alfie and his new found talent offered some respite from his sadness. Mr. Hare, the choirmaster, although demanding, was a kind old man who had a gentle way about him. He sensed that young Alfie, the new boy, was bewildered by his circumstances and tried his best to elicit some cheer from the child.

'Smile, Alfie Cattell,' he would sing, to the tune of whatever hymn they were currently practising. 'Have mercy on us, oh Great Lord, and make small Alfie smile.'

The other boys found this hilarious, but no smiles were extracted from Alfie.

'He misses his sister Sir,' announced one of the older boys, a friend of Billy, who had asked him to keep an eye on Alfie.

'She's his big sister and he misses her.'

Chapter 8

The Dublin Sisters

Weeks had passed since Catherine was torn from her brothers, and she remained unresponsive to those around her. So withdrawn was she that even the most hardened women of the workhouse softened in an effort to revive her heavy spirits.

'The poor girl! She's like the walking dead. I don't expect she'll be with us long so I don't,' said Bernadette.

'I think you're right Bernie,' Colleen declared.

'I think we've to do something to help her,' Bernadette pronounced decisively.

Bernadette and Colleen shared a bed with Catherine, together with two other women. The workhouse had been built to accommodate three thousand people, but now held twice that number, and it was necessary for inmates to share beds, and some were forced to sleep in the corridors.

The young girls often found it embarrassing to be crowded together with women of all ages, many of whom had been ladies of the night and were now too old and weary to make a living on the streets. Some were foul-mouthed and half-crazed. Catherine was afraid of them.

Colleen and Bernadette were sisters whose mother had fallen victim to the famine of 1878, which had cruelly visited the population of Ireland. They had come over on the boat from Dublin with their father, hoping for a better life. Their father, Paddy was a strong labourer and knew there was plenty of work to be found in the thriving city of Liverpool, but only days after their arrival he fell ill with fever and became too weak to earn the money needed to care for himself and his daughters. Distressed and desperate, he and the girls had been taken into the workhouse until he regained strength, but the meagre workhouse food rations made this a slow process. However, in spite of their predicament, Colleen and Bernie did not regard the situation as hopeless, merely temporary, and at least they were grateful to be together.

'Think what it must be like to be thrown into this place alone Colleen, like poor wee Catherine. No wonder she's hardly said a word since she came,' Bernadette lamented.

'Not a word' agreed Coleen, 'and not a thing we can do about it.'

The girls were picking oakum, fingers cut and sore from the loathed, laborious chore which involved pulling old ropes apart. The resultant fibres were put to use in various ways, one of which, ironically, was the stuffing of pillows for the inmates with their callused fingers, to sleep on.

'Sure it's her brothers she's fretting over, especially Alfie, the wee one. If she could only see him I'm sure she'd pick up a bit. It would do her the world of good,' Bernadette mused.

'I'm thinking we should have a wee word with the matron, you know Bernie. The girl will fret herself into the grave if we don't do something.'

Resolute, the sisters went about their task with a vigour seldom seen amongst workhouse inmates. Their hearts warmed in that cold, cheerless place, by the decision to help Catherine.

Matron dealt with numbers, not individuals; how many mouths to feed? How many beds were needed? How many plates? How much food? A new little girl became the needer of another pinafore, plate, bed, nightgown, dress. How could she care about loneliness, heartbreak or pain? Such was her mindset, when the two sisters approached with their request. They were not to know about the layers of numbers and needs which separated the matron from the rest of mankind.

The two 'needers' approached, smiling. This was unusual, matron was unaccustomed to smiles, and responded with a quizzical glare. Bernadette's courage faltered, but Colleen squeezed her hand.

'Matron, we've come to tell you about a wee girl in our dormitory, Catherine Cattell,' Bernadette ventured.

Matron's glare intensified. The girls stood close together, fragile reeds poised to withstand the tumult of her anger. Colleen squeezed Bernie's hand till it hurt.

'Cathy shares a bed with us.'

'How many in the bed?'

'Five matron,' Bernie replied counting on her fingers.

'Then there's room for another,' matron was victorious.

She reached for the notepad attached to string around her waist and made a note.

'Cathy hasn't eaten for two weeks and she cries all the time matron.'

'Which dormitory are you occupying?'

'Number ten.'

Bernadette began to feel hopeful. Matron was taking notes and showing an interest in Catherine.

'Are there any more beds in there with less than six occupants?'

'I don't know matron.' Bernie began to despair.

'We need another count.'

'Cathy could be dying matron. We think she's very ill,' Colleen added in desperation.

'What's her name again?' Matron asked wearily.

'Catherine Cattell.' Colleen's heart skipped a beat.

'Cattell? Ah yes, two brothers occupying a bed in the male quarters. Three Cattells in all.'

'That's right matron. She misses her little brothers so she does. We thought if she could see them she might...'

'Chapel.'

'Matron?' Colleen brightened.

'Take her to the Chapel. I believe there's a Cattell in the choir.' She dismissed the girls and hurried to find the janitor. A bed count was needed.

The girls left matron to her calculations, elated by the result of their audacious quest, and holding hands, they skipped back to the dormitory.

'Alfie's in the choir Cathy!' they chorused brightening the sombre chamber with their excitement.

On hearing his name Catherine gasped as if breathing for the first time. A sharp and sudden intake of stale workhouse air which served to render the first stirrings of a revival from the lonely half-life she had endured since the separation.

'The choir?' Catherine quizzed.

It seemed an odd word to hear in their present circumstances. The notion of a workhouse choir was one which Catherine would never have considered, were it not for the fact that Alfie's name was now attached to it.

'I didn't know Alfie could sing,' she murmured.

'Well he can, and we're going to hear him tonight, so we are,' Colleen chirped.

It was dark when the girls reached the chapel, chores complete and supper over. Colleen and Bernie glowed with excitement at their new friend's revival. Catherine had rallied at the thought of seeing her little brother again, and it occurred to her that she must not let Alfie witness her weakened state. It would help him if he knew she was strong and, although her appetite had not returned, she forced herself to eat the food she had of late, so vehemently rejected.

The three held hands as they approached the chapel, Bernie and Colleen, strikingly pretty with their flaming red hair and green eyes, were not cowed by their situation and Catherine, small and fragile, her pale face ghostly white in contrast walked between them gaining strength with every step.

In the cold winter darkness the candlelit chapel windows winked serenely as they approached and heard the slither of a song begin to penetrate the bleakness. The sisters felt Catherine's grip tighten around their hands as they entered the chapel.

Mr. Hare stood before the little group of choristers, pleased with their efforts in the damp, draughty chapel as they sang *The Holly and the Ivy* in preparation for the Christmas concert due to happen in two weeks time on Christmas Eve, when numerous city officials would gather, as well as many of the inmates. It was a bittersweet event which often tore at the emotions of the paupers, many of whom had enjoyed past Christmas' in better circumstances, and Mr. Hare was aware of the fact that the voices of his scraggy urchins had the power to melt the hardest of hearts.

In the half-light he pondered the boys' faces which, in the harsh light of day, carried scars of the hard knocks life had thrown at them, but were almost angelic as they sang their favourite carol and then, as they reached the last verse, he became aware of an odd, stirring amongst them as they began to nudge each other and look beyond him into the shadowy enclaves of the chapel. As he studied their faces for clues, he noticed something very strange in the ranks. There on the front row, he saw that sad little Alfie was smiling!

The three girls sat together on a wooden bench, which offered no degree of physical comfort, but the sight of her little brother looking well and smiling, gave Catherine all the comfort she needed. Mr. Hare did not prevent Alfie running to her at the end of practice and the two hugged so hard it hurt.

'Now Cathy, to be sure you can stop worrying about wee Alfie. He's in fine fettle,' Bernie sang, imitating the choristers, as they made their way back to the dormitory hand in hand.

They laughed at her effort to hold a tuneful note.

'I'll never, ever forget what you two did for us,' Catherine gushed, her face alight with joy and her voice reflecting the passion she felt for the girls and their kindness.

'Ah go on wit'ya Cathy. We only did what's right. You'd have done the same for us, so you would.' Colleen put her arm around Catherine's shoulders and the three workhouse inmates skipped back to the freezing dormitory as if they were residing in a palace.

Alfie ran back to the boys' quarters, grinning from ear to ear to tell Billy the news. He found him with his gang of friends, talking about the ships at the Pier Head and impressing them with his knowledge of all things nautical. His stories served to distract them from the misery of their plight and also planted the seed of desire for a life at sea in many of their shipwrecked lives.

'I saw Cathy!' Alfie bellowed, much to the annoyance of the gathering. They glared at him. He was flushed with excitement and looked different from the boy who left them two hours earlier.

'Cathy who?' Georgie Gibbs queried, reluctant to switch his thoughts from a life at sea with Billy, to the matter of a girl he didn't even know.

'My sister,' said Billy, trying to hide his elation from the boys who he knew admired him. Losing control of his emotions would seem unmanly, but being responsible for Alfie since they had been left in the workhouse had forced him to grow up sooner than he would have chosen. He was sensitive enough to know how badly Alfie was suffering, and although he had tried many ways to cheer him up, he knew that only Catherine could manage that, or better still, their father.

Billy left his friends and went to Alfie.

'She came to choir practice,' Alfie confided, calmer now.

'You mean she's in the choir too!' Billy responded, genuinely astonished by the thought.

'No! She came to watch me and she was with two girls, not alone.' Alfie's words tumbled out, putting an end to his prolonged sorrow.

Billy was so relieved to hear this that in spite of his friends watching, he gave his little brother a hug and ruffled his hair in celebration. The other boys, for a brief moment, dropped the manly facades, nodding and smiling at each other, extracting fragments of long lost joy from their friends' happiness.

Chapter 9

Miss Clancy

In the days after her reunion with Alfie, Catherine began to eat again and gain some strength, although the joy of that moment in the chapel with her brother would sustain her, there was little else to be joyful about. She realised how fortunate she was to have the support of Colleen and Bernadette and their optimism was a great comfort, but day to day life was filled with challenges, the routine relentless, from morning call at dawn, when she untwined herself from the tangle of arms and legs with which she shared the hard, narrow bed, to the time she collapsed back onto the bed and would be asleep before the last lamp was out. Often she would be sore and bruised after falling out of bed during the night, having been kicked or pushed by a sleeping companion.

There were some older women in their dormitory who were not in the habit of rising at dawn. They were rough characters whom Catherine avoided when possible. One in particular, Rosie, she feared. Rosie was well suited to her name, with long black hair, a white complexion, green eyes and striking red cheeks. At twenty-one, her vibrancy was dwindling and signs of premature ageing marred the beauty which had made her popular with the Lime St punters. Always defensive and ready for a fight, Rosy intimidated the younger girls. Catherine learned not to glance her way as, if she caught your eye she would confront you; 'Who are you luk'n at girl?' with an emphasised *you* she would poke the poor victim in the chest. 'Don't luk at me that way!' She would continue, poking with every word.

Having negotiated the avoidance of Rosy's glance at

dawn, the next trial was a cold water splash, which brought her fully awake.

Quickly donning the black dress and white pinafore workhouse uniform, she would join the other girls in making the bed and cleaning the dormitory, before leaving for breakfast; a dish of gluey porridge swilled down by cold water and taken in silence, together with row upon row of broken lives, young and old, each with their own sad story to tell.

After breakfast the children would have three hours of schooling but, as Catherine was nearly thirteen, she had been placed with the needlework teacher Miss Clancy, to learn a skill which would help her earn a living when she eventually re-joined the human race.

Colleen and Bernadette were assigned the same workshop, but they were forced to communicate through signs and eye motion. They were not permitted to talk as they sewed.

It was dull, repetitive work, stitching pinafores, pillowcases and dresses in the high-windowed room, and Miss Clancy, with her grey hair pulled back in a tight bun, encased in her stiff, black dress, examined every stitch made in the room for length and alignment. Ardently religious, she would command them; 'Stitch your prayers into the work girls, Jesus will be your salvation!'

If Miss Clancy found a wrong stitch, she would pull the whole seam out and throw the garment back for the terrified girl to begin again. Catherine took care with her stitching, but Bernie could never get it right, and occasionally she and Catherine secretly exchanged work so that Cathy could complete a neat row of stitches for her friend.

'You've save my life Cathy, so you have. Sure if old Clancy ever got a glimpse of my stitches, she'd have me hung out to dry for a heathen. There's no sign of Jesus in my efforts with the needle so there's not, more like the devil himself wouldn't you say?' Bernadette giggled.

'You could be right Bernie,' Catherine sighed. 'I don't think the devil can be too far from any place Miss Clancy is.'

'Don't let her get you down Bernie,' Colleen comforted.

The girls were working in the laundry that afternoon, loading bales of sheets and towels into vats of boiling water, hardly able to see each other through the thick billows of steam.

'But I'll never be able to sew a straight seam, so I won't,' wailed Bernie as she wafted the relentless steam, which settled and drenched her hair and clothes and stole silently into her lungs.

Catherine and Colleen, heaved the final bale of soiled linen into the vat and pushed it down with a huge wooden dolly, then dizzy with heat, the three walked to their dormitory through the bitter December cold. The fire was lit in their room, but Rosy and her friends huddled before it, like crows around their prey, preventing any warmth from circulating. The three perched on their bed to await the supper bell, but Bernadette, aching from the day's work, soon lay down and drifted off to sleep.

'Will you come with me to see Alfie after supper Colleen?' Catherine pleaded.

The chapel visits were now a nightly event, during the week before Christmas. Mr. Hare had allowed Catherine to stay and watch her brother and spend a few moments with him after each practice. Alfie was able to tell her about Billy and his friends and that at school he was doing well.

'We've been drawing Christmas pictures, and the Miss says I've got a talent,' he had announced, the day before.

Catherine treasured the moments with her little brother, and desperately wanted the family to be together again.

'Of course we'll come, sure a ticket on the ferry to Dublin wouldn't stop us, so it wouldn't,' Colleen joked.

The supper bell rang and they tried to wake Bernie, but she was sleeping soundly.

'Ah leave her be Cathy. Supper's nothing to sing about and she probably needs the sleep more. Let's be off now.'

They joined the throng of inmates making their way to the canteen. Many were elderly women, husbands long dead, who were no longer of use to their grown families and had no means of support. Some had enjoyed success in life, but when husbands or fathers were forced into bankruptcy, they had no other choice but to join the forlorn ranks.

Catherine searched their faces for a spark of hope. Sometimes she would detect it, the ones for whom this was a passing dark cloud behind which the sun waited, ready to shine on a better life sometime in the future. In others she saw only resignation and no sign of the energy needed to break free.

She desperately wanted to be one of the hopeful ones, even though there were times when escape seemed impossible, she clung to the thought that somewhere beyond the high walls which enclosed them, there was someone thinking about the three of them. Maude would never forget about them - that she knew for certain - and although there had been no word of her father for more than two years, she sensed he was alive and that in time he would come for them.

As the girls ate warm gruel in the eerie silence which befell the room while the weak, weary and hungry inmates relished their morsel, they regretted their decision to let Bernadette sleep. The warm meal would have been good for her and breakfast was such a scant affair that she would have trouble getting through the day tomorrow.

After supper they braved the cold and made their way to chapel. Mr. Hare was working the choir particularly hard in preparation for the carol concert on Christmas Eve and the Christmas Day services. He had insisted the boys eat well to build their strength for the effort ahead, and the girls were truly impressed by the results.

Afterwards Alfie spent a few moments with them and gave Catherine three pictures he had drawn at school, one for each of them.

'They're Christmas trees,' he explained, 'like the one we had in Great Newton St when mammy was alive, Cathy. I thought we could get one the same next year when we we're out.'

'We will Alfie, I promise we will.' She pulled her little brother close to her and wrapped him in her arms, burying her face in his hair. Where was their father? How could he let this happen? The thoughts tormented her. 'Next Christmas will be different Alfie, I promise.'

The girls sombrely made their way back to the dormitory. Above them an infinity of stars dazzled the dark December sky and a bright, full moon beamed blue streaks of light across their path;. Catherine's promise to Alfie had changed their mood and sewn a seam of determination into the fibres of each girl's being, so straight and perfect, that

Miss Clancy would be proud, and somehow they would both find a way to fulfil it.

In the lamplight of the cold room, where Rosie and her cronies huddles near the embers of a feeble fire in the hearth, the girls sensed something awful. A silver slither of moonlight cast its glow across the room and onto the empty bed where they had left Bernie sleeping.

'Where's my sister?' Colleen demanded.

'They took her away,' Rosy replied, reaching for Colleen and placing a hand gently on her shoulder.

'Sure, who took her away?' Colleen demanded. 'She's my sister!'

Chapter 10

The Man in the Shadows

The day Lizzie had taken the children to the workhouse, Maude had been at her grandmother's house on Peach St. She and Catherine often called in on their grandparents and busied themselves around the house, scrubbing the floors and doorstep and washing clothes and bed linen. Margaret Quirke was not, genetically speaking, their real grandmother, but since she had married their granddad long before they were born, she was accepted as such without question.

On the day it happened, Lizzie had asked Maude to go to Peach St with a basket of food she'd been busy baking.

'Your grandma's expectin' you Maudie, and I think she's want'n you to stay an help out with a few things.'

'Right mammy, I'll just get Cathy to come along.'

Maude and her mother were sitting at the table, in front of the hob peeling potatoes for supper. Lizzie had sent Catherine upstairs to clean the room, in which she slept, together with Maude, Billie, Alfie, and her younger cousins, Beatrice, Jack and Tom. A curtain draped across the room separated the boys and girls, but offered very little in the way of privacy.

'Cathy's stoppin' here today Maude. I have a few jobs for her,' Lizzie ventured.

'She can do them when she gets back Mam. I'll help her,' Maude responded cheerfully.

'No luv' you go, yer gran's waiting, Cathy's stoppin' here today.'

Maude became suspicious; her mother had threatened to take her cousins to the workhouse on a few occasions recently, saying she had reached, the end of her tether with it all, and couldn't manage to feed all the mouths in the house. She and Catherine had huddled together on the front step after one such outburst.

'Don't worry Cathy, I won't let her do it,' Maude had whispered. Catherine desperately searched the street for her father, as she always did from her lookout on the top step. She always believed he would appear at any minute and all would be well.

She turned to her mother, who was now fussing around the stove with a wet rag, scrubbing away at a non-existent stain. 'What are you planning mam?' Maude quizzed.

'Planning? What do you mean luv? I've got no plans for today beyond cleaning the house and cooking,' Lizzie responded with false breeziness.

'In that case Cathy can come with me,' Maude was defiant.

'I need her to stay here Maudie. She can keep an eye on the boys while I get a few jobs done. Time you were off now, grandma's waiting for you.'

Maude blamed herself for what happened to Catherine and the boys that day. In spite of her misgivings, she had left the house and her cousins at the mercy of her mother, whose behaviour had been worrying of late. There had been hushed conversations between her parents and although Maude knew the decision had not been easy for them, nevertheless, her closeness to Catherine would never allow her to concede that it was the right one.

On her return that day she found her mother in the best room, used only on special occasions, vigorously polishing the ornamental brassware displayed around the hearth.

'Where's Cathy, Mam?' she enquired, fearing the worst. Lizzie continued to buff the brass plate, as sunlight filtered through gauze curtains and a million tiny particles of dust floated aimlessly across shafts of light in that neat little room, reserved for special times like weddings, christenings and funerals.

'She's gone luv. I couldn't cope and we have no money Maudey! I had to do it, God knows I tried my best but it was impossible to carry on. You four need food and clothes. What was I to do? They'll be better off in the workhouse... fed, looked after. They'll be better off Maude. I know they will. They're my poor sister's children. I wouldn't do anything bad to them. I wouldn't!'

Maude noticed the redness around her eyes and knew her mother was suffering, but Catherine had gone and her life was destroyed.

'Mammy! We've got to get them back! Come with me now, Mam. Let's get them. It's not too late and we'll manage. Me and Cathy can work at something. Come on Mam let's go.' Maude rushed to fetch her mother's cape and bonnet as she spoke, and now stood hopefully before her mother, who remained on her knees and would not meet her gaze.

'It's done Maudie, It's done. That's the end of it!' Lizzie's tone was adamant; there would be no further discussion.

From that evening, Maude kept vigil at the workhouse gate, peering through iron railings into the grey, cobbled yard where often a waif of a girl aimlessly wandered.

'Have you seen Catherine?' Maude had called out hopefully.

'Catherine died today. She died,' the girl responded with an eerie vagueness that cast doubt on the truth of her statement.

'Catherine Cattell, I mean, with Billie and Alfie. Have you seen them?' Maude persisted.

'All dead.' Said the girl. 'We've all died.'

And off she drifted, a workhouse Ophelia, serving only to confuse the sad and desperate little girl on the other side of the gate.

Maude returned home and sat on the top step without Catherine beside her and, as the light faded on that cold October evening, she resumed Catherine's watch, ever hopeful that her uncle John would return.

For a while this was her routine; every day she would stand and wait at the gate, hopeful to catch a glimpse of her cousins or someone who knew them. Wrapped in a green woollen cape and wearing her red felt bonnet to shield her from the bitter wind, she would watch the yard, but it was not easily accessible for the inmates and, apart from the spectral girl whose morbid pronouncement had left her worried and bemused after the first visit, nobody else seemed to frequent that hidden corner of the yard. The only regular visitors were pigeons and sparrows, neither of which lingered long, since there was nothing to keep them there. Evenings saw her on the top step. Sometimes her little sister Beatrice would join her, and as they watched they would think of ways of finding Uncle John.

Beatrice, a sharp witted little girl of six years, was one of the fair-haired, blue-eyed members of the clan and, as her features emerged from the baby years, Maude was surprised to discover her little sister was the image of Catherine, and as she shared the top step with her, it was almost like having her cousin there beside her. Through Beatrice's companionship she began to feel less lonely.

Beatrice had been playing stick-and-hoop up and down the cobbles, and was quite adept at keeping the wooden hoop upright as she chased it down a slope in the road. When it wobbled and clattered onto the road, she retrieved it and joined Maude.

'Do you really think Uncle John will come back Maudie?' she asked, putting the hoop over her head and suspending it round her neck like a giant necklace. The lamplighter was doing his rounds and, as he lit the lamppost positioned outside their house, they huddled in its glow, Maude pulling Beatrice close to her.

'He has to Beatie. I can't think of any other way of getting them out of that awful place, unless Mam changes her mind, and that's not going to happen.'

'Why not write notes and tie them to trees, and everywhere? We could leave them at St George's Hall and all over the Pier Head. *Come Home John Cattell*!' Beatrice suggested.

Maude laughed at the idea.

'You write the notes Beatie my sweetie, and I'll come with you to do the sticking. How many will you make?'

'Five to start with,' Beatrice looked earnest. 'We'll tie them to all the lampposts on Great Newton St.'

'It'll be a start,' Maude nodded supportively.

While they were talking Maude was watching the figure of a man standing just beyond the lamplight across the street. She had not noticed him pass by, so he must have come from the Brownlow Hill end of their street. She would not have thought much of his presence, except that she remembered seeing a man in the same spot the two previous evenings. He had lingered for a while before walking back in the direction from whence he came. She squinted to get a clearer view through the darkness, but could not make out any features and, thinking there would be no harm in getting a closer look, she descended the steps. But before she reached the road, the man had gone. Deciding not to mention him to Beatrice, she climbed the steps to the front door and ushered her inside.

'Come on Beat it's too cold to be sitting here now.'

Instinct was telling her that something had changed. That in all the time she and Catherine had kept watch, this was a significant sighting, and as she joined her family, warm around the table in the kitchen, she wanted to believe that at last, Catherine's daddy had come home.

Chapter 11

Ann

There were pools of water in the yard beyond Maude's gate at the workhouse. She had come to regard it as her gate, since standing at it was now a regular part of her almost weekly routine. The rain had been relentless for two days and as darkness fell across Liverpool, Maude was about to end her vigil when the spectre girl appeared. She waded through the water seemingly oblivious to her drenched state. Reaching for the bars of the gate she clutched them, and Maude was surprised to perceive signs of intelligence in the gaze which met hers. They faced each other, divided by a few strips of wrought iron and a few degrees of poverty.

Close up the girl was older than Maude had guessed during their first brief encounter; possibly her own age, no longer a child, not quite a woman, ghostly pale with her green eyes conveying deep depths of sorrow.

'Have you seen Catherine?' Maude pleaded. The girl was silent. 'What's your name?' Maude ventured, hoping to gain her trust.

'Ann,' she replied, 'I'm Ann.'

It was as if she had spoken her name for the first time and was surprised to discover that she owned one.

'Ann, take this note and give it to Catherine.' Maude pulled Ann's wet fingers from the bar and wrapped them round the note she had written that morning. 'Please give it to Catherine,' she repeated as Ann waded back across the yard and out of sight. Maude doubted the note would reach her cousin, but it was worth a try, and as she splashed through the puddles on her way home, she allowed herself a few cautiously joyous big splashes.

Chapter 12

The Note

The puddles left by the rain had turned to ice by Christmas Eve, making the journey to chapel treacherous for the cold, feeble waifs and strays who struggled to remain upright on their way to the carol service. Attendance was obligatory for those able to manage the short journey, although there was a lack of Christmas cheer amongst their number.

Catherine and Colleen were numbed not only by the freezing temperature, but also by the events of the previous day. During their absence, Bernie had collapsed and been taken to the infirmary, and the girls had been unable to glean any information about her state of health.

'You'll just have to hope and pray,' the warden had sneered.

It transpired that Bernie had been found beside the bed, apparently lifeless, by Rosie, after supper.

'She was laid over there on the floor. White as a sheet she was, poor thing, and freezing cold. I put one of them blankets over her and sent Minnie to get help.' Rosie's characteristic harshness had dissolved as she recounted the events. 'I thought she was dead Collie, but then her eyes gave a tiny flicker and I pulled her close to me so as to warm her up a bit. Then matron came and they took her away.'

Catherine hated to see the anguish in Colleen's eyes and knew it would remain until she was together with her sister again. That night had been the cruellest either of them had experienced, as they lay awake listening to the hellish sounds of misery that pierced the darkness. In their threesome they had felt safe, but Bernadette's absence, and the terrible thought that it may be forever, had left them both in shock and trembling beneath the scanty bedclothes, they had clung to each other.

As they reached the chapel the next evening, an old woman approached, toothless and sallow skinned with wisps of grey hair tucked in a white mop cap. 'Are you Colleen?'

'I am that,' Colleen responded, intrigued.

'I've to tell you Bernie's awake and getting better.'

Her message delivered, she nodded and was about to walk away, but Colleen pulled her back and delivered a hug almost enough to break her feeble bones.

'Sure is that the truth?'

'Yes it is dearie. She told me with her very own mouth when I was up on her ward last night. The doctor says it's pneumonia, and she's very poorly, but by the grace of God, she'll get better.'

Her smile, even without teeth, lit up the ancient face.

'Will you see her again?' Catherine asked hopefully.

'I'll be back up there tonight girlie.'

'Please could you give her this?' Catherine dug into the pocket of her pinafore and pulled out the Christmas tree Afie had drawn for Bernie. The three observed it with delight. A watercolour, perfectly balanced tree, emblazoned with candles and baubles below which were the words *Happy Christmas Bernadette* in beautifully formed script. It occurred to Catherine that Alfie had inherited their father's artistic talent, as she noted the precision with which it had been drawn, and for a dizzying moment she remembered how Alf would perch on the chair arm watching their daddy sketch his designs for the print works.

'She'll get it tonight luvies. My name's Gertie, if you need to find me, just ask for Gertie the nurse.'

'Thank you Gertie.'

The girls chorused and the chapel bell rang for the service to begin.

Inside the chapel Mr. Hare's ragged choir delivered their songs to a forlorn congregation, but Alfie, perched on a bench on the second row, had a clear view of his sister who smiled proudly, like a mother watching her child at a school concert. Catherine saw that he was glancing from her to another area of the chapel and following his lead she looked across the aisle to where the men stood, a weary collection of skin and bones who at first glance were identical, wearing the same workhouse clothes, but to her delight and looking directly back at her from the end of the adjacent pew, was Billy, beaming at her.

'That's our Billy over there,' She whispered, nudging Colleen and twitching her head in his direction.

Colleen glanced across and found Billy, still grinning and looking directly at her, he was pointing to the person next to him, and when Colleen met the gaze of the tall, shock-haired man beside him, her knees gave way and to Catherine's horror she collapsed onto the bench.

'Collie! What is it?'

'It's me Da.'

The people around them unperturbed by the drama, droned on with a melancholy rendering of *Away in a Manger.*

Paddy McGuire had endowed his children with his own good looks, and stood out amongst the inmates as a man passing through. Although, still in her rapturous state, Colleen noticed a drastic weight loss in her once strong and powerfully built father, but she nevertheless, saw that he was in good spirits as he winked across at her.

After the service, the strict rules of segregation were relaxed so that family members could have a brief reunion, before being herded back to their respective blocks.

The only warmth outside emanated from the lips of the cruelly separated men, women and children.

'Da, have you heard about Bernie?' Colleen cried as she reached for his hand, slithering unsteadily on the icy cobbles.

'I have, to be sure, Coll.' Paddy held her close to him. 'They let me see her this morn'n, so they did, and you've not to worry, she'll be well enough, soon enough. What about youself?'

'I'm grand now I've seen you Da. This is Cathy Cattell, my great friend.'

'Billy and Alfie's big sister, to be sure!' Paddy grinned.

Catherine, Billy and Alfie were standing together, the boys encircled by Catherine's embrace.

'They're brave little fellas Cathy, don't be worrying your head about the boys now. I have a note for you from Bernie.'

To Catherine and Colleen's surprise, Paddy reached into

his pocket and pulled out a grimy piece of folded paper.

'She said I was to pass it to you. A bit of a strange girl called Ann had been calling your name around the wards, and sure, when Bernie said she knew you, she gave her this note. Bernie didn't want Gertie the nurse to have it, as she thinks it's special, and she was saving it to give you herself, but I told her I was going to the chapel for the carols with the hope of seeing you both, so she left it with me.'

The call went out for them to return to their quarters. Catherine took the mysterious note from Paddy's huge hand and held it tight in her palm; she felt the time was not right to read it. Before they parted, Paddy took Colleen by the shoulders; 'Collie, I'm feel'n stronger now, so I am, and I've been out looking for work. There's plenty of it down at the docks and I'll be leaving this God forsaken place soon.'

Colleen's blue eyes filled with tears, which spilled onto her abundantly freckled, ice cold cheeks.

'I'll come and fetch you when I find a place to live, my pretty wee girl, so don't fret.'

The wardens, having exhausted their ration of Christmas cheer, moved in to herd them away, so they said their goodbyes, carefully negotiating the treacherous terrain to make their way back, as darkness fell on Christmas Eve. It wasn't until they reached their dorm that Catherine could unfurl the damp wedge of paper and, in a softly golden lamplight, was just able to read the words:

My dearest Catherine,
Do not despair; I will wait at the cobbled yard
gate to see you every afternoon at four o'clock.
I think your daddy has returned.
Your beloved cousin,
Maude

It had been a day of surprises for both girls, but when Catherine read Maude's note to Colleen the two were speechless for some time. The other occupants of their room were gathered around the hearth talking about Christmas and how awful it was to be in the workhouse instead of with family.

'My mam made plum pudding like no-one else,' Eve

Smith mused, gazing dreamily into the dying embers, the child emerging briefly from a cocoon of world weariness, spun over years of hardship. 'There was ten of us children and always enough food to go round. She'd spin in her grave if she knew I was in here, an' if it weren't for that stupid husband of mine and his gamblin' I would 'ave been making my own plum pudding now.'

The others joined in with a stream of similar stories and romantic memories of wonderful Christmas' past. Catherine and Colleen were in bed, oblivious to the seasonal banter, while they continued to study Maude's note, seemingly searching for more; another clue to cast light upon her final sentence.

Colleen could still sense the warmth of her father's hands and smiled as she remembered his defiant wink in the chapel. Where there was so much misery and self-pity, her da and Cathy's brother Billy, reminded her that this was not forever, and there was a life beyond the workhouse gates, where she would be very soon, and now this; could there really be the same hope for Cathy and her brothers? Had their da come to fetch them?

Chapter 13

Christmas Day

'I need to see Maude,' Catherine finally announced, returning from the depths of thought into which the note had carried her.

'Yes but four in the afternoon's not a good time to get away and where's the gate at the cobbled yard?'

'I've been thinking about that and wonder if she means the traders' entrance, where supplies get delivered. It's walled off from the rest of the workhouse, but there's a door that's sometimes left open. We'll go along tomorrow. I'm desperate to see her and even more desperate to hear what she has to say about my daddy.'

After lights out and the usual scramble for space in their bed, neither girl slept for a long time, with thoughts of escape, and having a real life, racing through their heads.

The workhouse on Christmas Day was not a joyous place to be, although an effort was made to bring a modicum of cheer. Walls were hung with coloured paper chains made by the inmates, and Christmas dinner was served to the tightly packed rows of hungry, cheerless individuals, all of whom would rather be elsewhere. There were those however, who were grateful to have shelter, food and warmth, in spite of the circumstances, and the day was markedly different from others, by the fact that they had no work to do.

A warmer rain had fallen overnight leaving only traces of the ice which had caused a number of casualties to be carried off to the infirmary. After dinner, the inmates were given free time, and many gathered in day rooms to tell stories and sing Christmas songs; there was an unusual outpouring of love and camaraderie. The girls sensed a significant change of mood in the normally severe wardens, and wondered if they might be able to take advantage of the occasion.

They were sitting together on a bench in the women's day room, a draughty place, where only the immediate vicinity of the hearth retained any degree of warmth. The Christmas dinner had been a treat, which both acknowledged, and the boost to their energy seemed also to have boosted their confidence.

'If you were given two wishes for Christmas Colleen, what would they be?'

'Well now. The obvious one would be to get out of this place.' Colleen's expansive gesture made Catherine smile.

'But, sure, it's not a possibility today. I think we need two wishes we can actually make true. What do you think, my friend?'

'And what would they be?'

'Well now, there just happen to be two people we both want to see, and it might just be possible to do so. What about we sneak into the infirmary and wish Bernie a happy Christmas, then wait at the cobbled yard gate to see if Maude arrives?'

Catherine thought for a while, observing weary women gathered in the dusty room beneath festive paper chains made by the inmates and hung around the workhouse; yellow, purple and scarlet, unusual in the institution where brown, blue and white dominated.

'Let's do it!' she finally ventured. 'If we go now to the infirmary, we should be able to make the gate at four o'clock.'

Chapter 14

The Itch Ward

The City of Liverpool was fighting a losing battle with the monstrous killer tuberculosis, which visited most households irrespective of class. There were also frequent outbreaks of typhoid, and many bronchial diseases caused by the polluted smog that frequently stood immovable and unwelcome around the streets and docklands. Wards in the infirmary were filled with the sick and dying, and those who worked there were also at risk of contracting a contagious death sentence.

As part of the workhouse complex, the entrance to the infirmary could be accessed by inmates, but visitors were not allowed, besides which only the foolish or desperate would want to enter. The girls slipped into the lobby without challenge. There was a minimum of staff present, and those on duty had no time to guard doors.

They knew that Gertie worked on the itch ward and hoped to find her there, but the size of the place was overwhelming and they were soon lost amid a warren of stairwells and endless corridors,

'We'll never find our way out of here Cathy. So we won't,' Colleen fretted.

They peered into wards where row upon row of beds yielded little comfort to their skeletal occupants. Catherine noticed the obligatory paper chains hanging limply amidst the misery; miniscule attempts at cheer.

They reached the fifth floor, spent with exertion and nausea, when Catherine saw a sign directing them to the itch ward.

'This is it Collie. Now what?'

Before Catherine had time to challenge her, Colleen pushed open the door and strode in, as if she had done so every day of her life. Within seconds of doing so, the nausea increased as she was unprepared for the sight of people terrorised by skin diseases which gave no respite. Catherine, less bold, crept in and stood shivering beside her. Their appearance brought a welcome distraction from the monotony of the day, and eyebrows rose around the ward.

'I think you might be lost.'

There was amusement in the tone of the voice which eventually emerged from a shadowy corner of the room. Laughter, instantaneous and unanimous, sprang from long untapped depths of submerged humour as the patients studied the two terrified young girls who looked as if they had entered a den of lions.

To their relief Gertie, startled by the strange behaviour of her patients, came running from the nurses' office. 'What's 'appeningere?' she exploded, her yellow face turning a deep shade of pink. 'What in evan's name are you two doin' 'ere?'

'We want to see Bernadette, Gertie. It's Christmas Day and I want to see my sister.'

'What do you think this is, an 'otel?' Gerie shrieked.

There was laughter around the ward again and the girls were mortified. Catherine saw that Colleen was close to tears and she wanted to run fast to get away from the spectacle of their disgrace.

'Where is she?' The voice from the corner queried.

'She's in the chest ward,' Gertie answered. 'Pneumonia.'

'Where's that?' Catherine queried, regaining her confidence and addressing the sympathetic voice in the shadows.

'End of the corridor, turn right and you're there,' said the mystery voice.

''ere, I'll take you,' Gertie offered. 'You lot behave yourselves, I'll be back in a whisker.'

As they left the ward the girls glimpsed the red and swollen face of the woman in the shadows.

'Thank you,' Catherine whispered, shocked by the sight.

'What's your name?' asked the woman.

'Catherine Cattell.'

There was a brief pause.

'John's daughter?' The woman responded.

'Yes. Do you know him?' Catherine was stunned.

'Know him? I did once, or thought I did. He told me about you and your brothers. He didn't forget you,' the woman said softly.

'How do you know him? Where is he now?' Catherine reeled with the shock of hearing her father's name.

'I don't know where he is. He may be dead for all I know.' The harshness had returned.

'Come on if you're coming,' Gertie shrilled, and ushered the girls out before Catherine had time to question further.

She was still dazed by the encounter when they reached the chest ward, where they found Bernie sitting up in bed looking frail but still breathing at least. She gasped with delight when she saw Colleen and Catherine enter the ward and the three hugged each other.

'For the love of God Bernie, we thought you'd died on us so we did.' Colleen was tearful as she clung to Bernie's hand.

'Well I have to say, I thought the same for a while,' Bernie smiled.

'Happy Christmas!' Colleen beamed, having fulfilled her wish and oblivious to the gloomy environment of the ward. Her sister was alive and she could hold her hand. That's what mattered.

Catherine noticed Alfie's Christmas tree picture beside Bernie's pillow.

'Tell him thanks for that. Whenever I'm feeling miserable I look at it and it cheers me up, so it does.' Bernie smiled, taking the picture and admiring the cheerful image, incongruous in her present surroundings. Colleen felt complete again at the sound of her sister's lovely voice, the absence of which had left a terrible void in her life. 'He's quite an artist your Alfie.'

Catherine nodded absently, her mind wandering to the strange woman in the itch ward. If only she'd been able to stay and ask more about her father, she may have been closer to finding him.

A large nurse was making her way towards them,

wearing an expression unsuited to the festive occasion.

'You'd better get out of 'ere,' Gertie advised in a loud whisper,

'It's Nurse Peg, not to be trifled with,' Gerie warned.

And turning to the girls she assumed an air of outrage, hands on hips and shouted; 'I telled yous two to get out now didn't I?'

The girls fled, leaving Bernie to explain their presence to Nurse Peg and wound their way through the maze of bleak corridors, before creeping out and into the half-light as the sun set. A crimson sky blazed above the workhouse, and the girls shivered.

They were so relieved to be out of the dreadful hospital atmosphere, thick with the smell if sickness and death, and able to breath the fresh icy air of freedom - albeit workhouse freedom - that their next wish had been forgotten and not until the chapel bell rang four times to mark the hour, did they remember Maude.

They sped to the little tradesman's courtyard and Maude's gate. Catherine stood on the lower bar and peered over the rails, up and down Brownlow Hill.

'She's not here. We've missed her,' she murmured despondently, shivering in her cotton pinafore, too flimsy to protect against the freezing December chill. Colleen climbed up beside her, still elated having seen Bernie, but feeling her friend's disappointment.

'She'll be back tomorrow,' Colleen comforted.

'Tomorrow we'll be working,' Catherine replied flatly.

The gas lighter was doing his rounds and glanced at them piteously as he passed. Catherine was reminded of the time she had passed the same gate with her mammy and daddy, many years earlier in what seemed to be another life, and was shocked at the sight of two sorrowful girls peering out at her. Now she and Colleen stood in their place.

Chapter 15

The Girls on the Step

Liverpool had hardly noticed his return as the population shivered and slithered through that cold December, but for John, the decision to leave Knowle, where Mary had gently restored him back to health, had been one of the hardest he had made. He was sure his children were in good hands, being cared for by Ann Marie's family. They had no need for him, the father who deserted them, who should have been stronger. But he needed to see them once more.

On his return he had found work with a shipping line, creating posters to advertise their ships' passage. A ship called *The Liverpool Lady* was due to leave for New York in February. A new life in America was appealing and he had decided to buy a ticket as soon as the company paid him, but he knew he could not leave England without seeing his children. A glimpse would suffice, no more than a glimpse.

As he watched the girls on the step from the shadows, time melted and the two year separation could have been no more than two weeks. Catherine had not changed. Maude had grown and seemed so much more mature, but his Catherine was just as he remembered her. He waited for a while but there was no sign of Billy or little Alfie, and when Maude appeared to look in his direction, he moved away, satisfied that Catherine, at least was safe.

He had found lodgings in a temperance boarding house near the river, and spent his evenings amongst the myriad of hopefuls arriving with carpet bags and boxes of belongings, ready to board a steamer to America. The scene at the Pier Head was festive, with fires burning in braziers, tin whistlers livening up the night while drunken sailors and Irish revellers danced beneath the silver moon, which all too soon would watch them dance on a faraway shore.

He knew a bit about the passage to America, and the risks these people faced, but he knew also that the sweet scent of hope was enough to carry them forward, in spite of the dangers at sea.

He watched young sailors preparing the ships' rigging and sails, and thought about Billy. He would be eleven now, old enough to go to sea. Would he be amongst these lads? He was afraid he may see him and not know him, his own son. He was afraid that Billy would not want to know him and the thoughts often led him to the bars he once frequented, filled with painful memories.

Once an old acquaintance recognised him; 'John Cattell! Are you a ghost? We thought you were long dead.'

'Not yet.' John smiled.

'Good to know it. There's enough death around without you joining the ranks,' the gruff old lag joked.

John moved on, not wanting the intimacy of conversation.

Every evening he looked for Billy. Knowing he was unlikely to find him amongst the crowds, but the fantasy of a joyous reunion would not leave him. Then, thinking about the girls on the step, and his bewilderment at Catherine's unchanged appearance, he felt a truth creeping in through the frost and freezing darkness of night. The little girl must not be Catherine. She must be one of Lizzie's younger daughters and if that was the case, where were his children?

JANUARY 1890

Chapter 16

A Sad Farewell

'Sure it won't be for long Cathy. I know me Da' will do something to help you and your brothers so he will.'

Bernie and Colleen were leaving the workhouse. The New Year had brought good news for their father, who had been given work as a navvy, building the railway. He had found lodgings in a shared house on Scotland Rd, near the docks, and was ready to gather his family around him.

'We'll be at the gate for you every day Catherine. Be sure of that. I didn't think I'd have regrets about leaving this place, but saying goodbye to you is truly hard.' Colleen wiped away a tear.

They were gathered in front of a meagre fire which flickered forlornly in the dormitory hearth. Matron would be collecting the sisters as soon as their father arrived and the formalities finalised.

'I'll think about you every day, whatever I'm doing here, I'll think about how we did everything together and how you cheered me up.' Catherine's pallid features, flanked by strands of fine fair hair reflected the helplessness of her situation. For her there was no way out, no father working hard to bring his family home, only a lost, rumour of a man who Maude saw standing in the shadows.

'Right lasses, yer dad's 'ere for you. Get yer stuff and say goodbye to the werkouse,' matron shrilled.

The girls hugged and left their friend, as the freedom they longed for beckoned, while their hearts felt heavy with sorrow for Catherine.

She couldn't bring herself to go to the gate, did not

want to see her friends on the other side watching her, and the days were filled with the mechanics of a meaningless life.

The routine became a vortex and sucked her energy so that she no longer went to watch Alfie in the choir. She got up in the dark, cold mornings, picked oakum till her fingers bled sat alone stitching in Miss Clancy's classes, and returned to bed in the cold dark night.

It was Gertie the nurse who broke through the cocoon within which Catherine was entrenched.

January brought milder weather and a welcome thaw rid weary streets and houses of the hardened crust of snow which seemed to have become a permanent feature. Gertie found Catherine in the oakum yard, her callused hands tugging at a thick length of old rope to separate the fibres.

'There you are girlie!' Gertie bellowed. ''Yer a 'ard one to find.'

'I'm here every day Gert,' Catherine responded. There was something about Gertie that lifted her spirits. The woman led a truly miserable existence and yet she emanated a stubborn resilience to hardship and managed, in her rough, gruff way to remain as a cheerful beacon of light on a fog laden horizon.

'Well me girlie. I've come with some news for you from 'Ellen in the itch ward.'

'Ellen?' Catherine asks.

'She what knows yer dad.'

'Is that her name Gert. I didn't know. So what's the news?' Catherine's cocoon was not about to be so easily penetrated.

'She says yer to look in *The Crown* on Lime St. But be quick because 'e's got a ticket to America.'

'And how am I s'posed to do that?' Catherine shrugged and continued her task.

'Not my problem girlie!' Gertie swooped out as swiftly as she had swooped in and the cocoon had weakened just a fraction.

Three weeks had passed since Bernie and Colleen had left her. Only three weeks? It seemed like three life-times. She thought about their parting words; 'We'll be at the gate every day,' and hoping they had not given up on her, she regretted having almost given up on herself.

After supper she went to the yard and peered through the railings at busy Brownlow Hill where the early evening socialites were about their business. Carriages carrying the very rich bumped along the cobbled road towards the city centre, where entertainment of the highest rank awaited them at theatres, music halls and restaurants. Liverpool was the second city to London and home to many wealthy merchants who enjoyed a charmed life in landscaped mansions on the city outskirts, where the sullied arms of smoke and grime could not reach.

Catherine was indifferent towards these people. She liked to see the beautifully groomed horses and polished carriages, but her thoughts never drifted to greater depths. She accepted that she was not one of them, and that was the end of it.

'So there y'are Cathy me darlin!' Her world warmed at the sound of Colleen's melodic voice. 'It's standin' here every night we've been and after frettin' our socks off about you,' Colleen scolded, but the girls joined hands through the railings, knowing that no such barrier could hinder their friendship.

Bernadette and Colleen looked stunning, with bright red shawls and emerald green bonnets to brighten their plain brown frocks. Long fiery curls hung in ringlets the like of which would never be seen on Catherine's side of the railings.

'Gertie gave me a message from Ellen in the itch ward,' Catherine whispered.

'Ellen?' The girls were puzzled.

'Yes, she knows my daddy.'

'Ah, sure the one you spoke to when we were about looking for Bernie,' Colleen recalled their Christmas visit to the infirmary with a smile.

'She says to look in *The Crown* on Lime St, and he's got a ticket to America.'

'America! Jaysus! I'll ask me Da to look for him. *The Crown* on Lime St's not the sort of place ladies like us should be hang'n around, so it's not,' said Bernie with a wink. 'More for the ladies of the night, to be sure.' Colleen swung her purse and affected a provocative walk to make her point. The three laughed hysterically until the bell rang for Cathy to return to her dormitory and destroying the mirth.

'Stay strong now Cathy! You'll soon be out here with us, havin' a laugh!' Colleen comforted.

'See you tomorrow?' Catherine pleaded.

'We will that!' Bernie promised.

But it would be a while, and under very different circumstances, before the three were to meet again.

Chapter 17

Billy

When Paddy McGuire left the workhouse he promised Billy Cattell that he would look out for some work for him; he knew it was Billy's ambition to go to sea, and saw no reason why a healthy lad of almost twelve should not be on his way to earning a living.

'I'll ask around the docks for you Billy lad,' he told his young friend as he left, and true to his word, Paddy found him work as a ship's hand. Billy stayed at the workhouse for a bed to sleep in, but now he was able to spend his days around the place of his dreams. He had been ten years of age when Auntie Lizzie left him in the workhouse, and he felt betrayed and bitter. The hurt as deep as the oceans he longed to sail and the hatred he had long nurtured for his father, like a dormant sea monster, submerged, awaiting an awakening, although those who knew him would never have believed him capable of such feelings. He was a warm and likeable boy whose cheerful, mischievous spark had not been extinguished by the suffocating regime he had endured.

Handsome and quick to smile, he was popular and made many friends among the inmates; friendships forged in adversity and strong enough to last a lifetime. But the memory of scouring the bars of Liverpool with Catherine and Alfie in search of their father, to bring him home for their dying mother, would never leave him, and although the longing to find his father remained, he knew he would never forgive him for deserting them.

The boat was a bright red steamer called *The Coral*, which carried passengers from Liverpool to Dublin. Tom

Featherstone, the Captain, was always looking out for lads "with the sea in their blood" as he put it, and sensed that Billy was just that.

'You're no stranger to the life here Billy,' he had remarked. 'I've watched you at the rigging, you know what you're doing!'

'I spent my childhood here Captain. Wanted to learn everythin' so I could be a seaman.'

'Work hard for me Bill and soon I'll take you on a trip. I like to keep the ship clean and tidy. If we look after her, she'll look after us.'

'I'll do me best Captain,' Billy replied, welling with joy.

In his bed at the workhouse, he felt the faint stirrings of hope, a new sensation, like life returning to a long numbed limb,

On *The Coral*, he cleaned the deck, polished brass and mahogany, checked the rigging and waved her on her way like a proud father as she bobbed, bright red on the choppy River Mersey.

It was on one such occasion in early February, after watching *The Coral* until she was a tiny dot on the churning waves of the Irish Sea, that he turned shivering towards the bustle of the Pier Head. It was early morning and Liverpool was already wide awake. The city was booming; hotels and guest-houses were full with travellers passing through, and every inch of land was claimed for development. Magnificent buildings dwarfed the people who flooded in their masses to find sanctuary at the gateway to a future that Liverpool had become. A magnet for artists, writers, architects, merchants and tradesmen, it had been named; *The Centre of the Universe* and, as Billy stood at the riverside that gusty February morning, he inhaled the pure excitement of the city and now that he belonged to a boat, and Captain Featherstone's crew, he felt he was part of it all and not a mere onlooker.

He watched for a while as the centre of the universe milled around him, and considered approaching the captain of *The Liverpool Lady* which was in dock and bound for America in ten days. It was his ambition to join a big ship one day, but the time was not right. Cathy and Alfie needed him.

It was in that moment, as his thoughts drifted to his

brother and sister that he saw the face. It emerged from the crowd, passed him and was gone. It was his father's face. The one he had searched for while his mother lay dying, the one he had dreamed about during the hopeless nights in the workhouse. It was thinner, greyer, but it was the same one!

'Daddy!' He called. 'Daddy!' But his father had gone. The crew of a Russian merchant ship had disembarked and swamped the pier, and Billy's daddy was lost again.

Chapter 18

Colleen

'Well if it's not Billy Cattell! Sure me Da said I'd find you around here, so he did. You're lookin' well Billy.'

It took a few moments for Billy to recognize the flame-haired girl standing before him. He had seen Colleen only once, in the workhouse chapel on Christmas Day, and then she was wearing the drab workhouse uniform. Here she was now flaunting a green velvet bonnet and cape, with a smile as broad as the River Mersey across her freckle strewn face. It was the smile that reminded him.

'Colleen?'

'That's me, so it is. I'm after lookin' for you. Me Da sent me Billy. Gertie the nurse sent him a note from Ellen in the itch ward to say that your Da's here and he has a ticket to America. So he has.'

'Gertie?' Billy puzzled.

'Yes Gertie, to be sure.'

'And Ellen in the itch ward?'

'Yes Ellen. She's a friend of your Da, or was. She says your Da hangs out at *The Crown* on Lime St, so he does, and you've to meet me Da there tonight.'

Billy was mesmerized by the vision that was Colleen and her lively Irish lilt. The message was secondary to the seed which had embedded itself at the core of his being. And there he stood at the centre of the universe, belonging to a little red ship called *The Coral*, knowing his dad was alive and not far away, but most significantly of all, he had fallen in love with Colleen.

Chapter 19

Rosie's Advice

The night of her meeting with Bernie and Colleen at the gate, Catherine developed a fever, crying deliriously into the darkness of the freezing room, her hot breath forming clouds of condensation.

It was Rosie who came to her bed and carried her limp, feather-light body swamped with fever to the infirmary. Rosie stayed with her and sponged her with cool water.

In the morning Catherine awoke to find the young woman who had terrorised her life during the early days of her workhouse confinement, sleeping exhausted on the floor beside her bed.

'Wake up young lady.' The tone was kind and the nurse gently stroked Rosie's head. 'Your patient is going to be fine.'

Catherine was weak but the fever had gone, leaving in its stead a bond of friendship between the two strong enough to last a life time.

'Don't mind me Cathy. I'm a woman of the night, It's all I know! But it'll be different for you. You'll have a better life.'

'Right now Rosie, life's not looking too great for either of us,' Catherine observed.

Seven years older and infinitely more world weary, Rosie assumed a motherly roll towards the girl whose life she had undoubtedly saved that night in February, and Catherine found that beneath the rough, defensive exterior lay a good nature, and a willingness to listen to her story.

'I'm sorry your mam passed away, Cathy, and your dad disappeared, but you've got some good memories and that's an 'elp. Your dad'll come back, I know he will. But if he doesn't, you'll be fine, I promise.'

Rosie's resolve strengthened Catherine and she emerged from her illness a changed person. Those words; "If he doesn't, you'll be fine," became her cornerstone. It had never occurred to her that she could move on from this misery, without her father rescuing her. But if Rosie had no such dream, why should she?

Chapter 20

Hope in Hats

Miss Clancy was pleased to see Catherine return to the sewing room after weeks recovering in the infirmary. She recognised talent in her pupil, whose work had always been outstanding.

'Catherine dear, how nice to see you back,' Miss Clancy gushed.

'Thank you Miss.'

Catherine's response was cautious. She had witnessed Miss Clancy's darker side when dealing with girls, like Bernie, who were not so good at stitching, and consequently, she had a terrible fear of being on the receiving end of the pious woman's wrath.

'I have a proposal for you my dear. Don't look so afraid, it's a good proposal. I have a friend who is a milliner. She is seeking an apprentice; someone able to wield a needle, and I've already secured you the position. You will start on Monday in her divine little shop which is situated on Church St. It will be a trial for two weeks which I am confident you will pass, after which you will lodge above the shop while in receipt of your training and a small stipend. Now you may resume your work.'

Miss Clancy permitted herself to smile briefly and Catherine, dizzy with shock, silently returned to the seat she had occupied for two years, stitching seams, which would stretch the length of the Mersey and then again for Bernie. She had never experienced sheer elation, but now it welled up from some dark untapped depth within her, and she wanted to scream with joy. But instead she fought back tears and stitched her joy and prayers of thanks into her work, just as

Miss Clancy had always instructed.

'You'll be makin' 'ats for posh people.' Rosie declared on hearing Cathy's news. 'That's what milliners do.'

'But I've only ever sewed a seam. I've no experience of hats.' Catherine had a sudden memory of her mother scolding her for calling a hat an 'at. 'Don't drop aitches Cathy, it's common,' she had warned her. Perhaps my mother had a premonition that I'd work in a hat shop, Catherine mused, she smiled at the thought.

''ats are more interestin' than seams luvy. All them feathers and lace. When I get out of 'ere I'll come and get an 'at you've made. Black an' red with an enormous brim.'

Rosie had placed a shabby pillow on her head and tied it with a piece of string she found in her pocket.

'I hope it won't be long before you're out Rose. Come and see me when you can.'

'I don't think your posh boss will want the likes of me in the shop, but I'll get a message through and if anyone gives you any trouble, let me know. I'll deal with them.'

'I'm sure you will Rosie, but I'd rather talk myself out of trouble thank you.'

'Please yourself then. But if anyone 'arms you sweetie, they'll answer to me.' Rosie strode off to her bed.

Catherine was so elated to be moving back to the world of the living, that she had not given much thought to her little brothers. Restless in her bed, she was aware that not only was her life about to be transformed, but this was an opportunity that could enable her to make plans for a future which would include Alfie and Billy. She recalled Rosie's wise words; "If your father doesn't return, you'll be fine." And now it seemed that, thanks to Miss Clancy, arch enemy and persecutor of all those wretched souls who struggled to sew a straight seam, she may indeed, be fine.

Chapter 21

Scotland Road

The workhouse committee had allowed Billy to leave the premises during the day on the basis that Captain Featherstone would pay for his keep until he returned from Dublin, whereupon he would enlist the boy as an apprentice on *The Coral*. Soon *The Coral* would be his home. Billy had no intention of staying on land for long, once his life at sea began. However, he was under obligation to return before six in the evening, after which time he would lose his right to stay and would be forced to spend the night sleeping on the streets.

'I can't go to *The Crown* to find my dad Colleen. I have to be back at the hellhole by six, else they'll lock me out and the Captain has paid my keep.'

They were making their way to Scotland Rd where Paddy and the girls lived.

'Sure, how will he know who your Da is? He's never seen the man. But I'm worried what he might do when he finds him, so I am. Your Da's not his favourite person, after what he did to you three.'

'He's not exactly mine either,' Billy lamented.

They had reached the house and were pushing past a gang of bedraggled, bony boys lurking round the doorstep. The place was teeming with people. Women with pasty babies on their arms, stood aimlessly around the hallway exchanging banalities to pass the time. Small barefoot children charged up and down the stairs, and on the landing men in suits solemnly smoked pipes, dignified in adversity.

'This is our place. Come on in.'

Colleen had opened a door on the ground floor at the front of the house and they entered a large, neat room. The furniture was shabby but sufficient. At one end of the room a curtain separated the living space from the beds, and in a dark alcove stood a stove and sink. Billy marvelled at it.

'Is it all yours?' He gasped.

'Mine and me Da and Bernie's. But Bernie must have gone off somewhere. Sure I thought she'd be here to say hello. Da's workin' But he'll be home soon Billy, will I get you a drink of water?'

'I have to be going Colleen.'

He felt suddenly shy, finding himself in a room alone with the girl to whom he had just given his heart even though she did not yet know it. He felt his cheeks begin to burn.

'I'll tell me Da you can't come tonight. Now I know where y'are I'll come and see you again.'

'I hope you do Colleen.'

The two parted but not without an exchange of significant glances, which left them in no doubt that their souls were now as one.

He made his way through the chaos of life in the docklands, where it seemed the nationalities of all the world had come together for a great gathering; Russians, Poles, Irish, Scottish, Italian, and Chinese mingling together and communicating as best they could. A brisk wind blew smoke from street fires, which welcomed any traveller to stop and catch some heat.

The memory of his father's face in the crowd returned to him. His unexpected passion for Colleen had temporarily erased the incident from his mind, but Billy knew it was only a matter of time before he would be reunited with the man for whom he felt only loathing.

Chapter 22

The Liverpool Lady

His feet ached through restless wanderings around the streets of Liverpool, and the turmoil of his thoughts found no peace in the city where his mind was haunted by the memory of his wife Ann Marie, and his cowardly abandonment of Catherine, Billy and Alfie.

John's decision to buy a ticket to America had been spontaneous, a sudden gesture which he felt would erase the past and allow him a new beginning. So now he walked and walked, anxious for his new life to arrive and for *The Liverpool Lady* to carry him away.

When Billy saw him at the Pier Head, John had been for his daily visit to *The Liverpool Lady*, the only place he was able to cease his wanderings. A gaunt figure, swamped in his long oversized greatcoat, seemingly oblivious to everything but the ticket in his pocket and the ship on which he was soon to sail.

Shame had prevented him from any attempt to contact his children or Ann Marie's family. He had persuaded himself that they were better off without him, and decided to ignore the voice of his conscience, which was bidding him to try harder and at least locate the children before sailing.

On his arrival in Liverpool he had lodged for a few nights at *The Crown* on Lime St, a busy gathering place for travellers and locals, but moved to a small guest-house further out of the city, when he noticed furtive glances cast his way through the smoke filled room, from a couple of seasoned drinkers slouched with pints and pipes at the bar.

One of the men happened to be the brother of Ellen, the poor woman languishing on the itch ward suffering from a serious case of scabies. She had befriended John during his time of turmoil, before leaving Liverpool, and it was through her brother that Ellen had learned of John's return and his intention to sail.

Gertie, the nurse, rented a small dank room in a house on Scotland Rd where she slept on a bundle of blankets. The kind old soul hastened to Paddy's lodgings with Ellen's message, and it became a race against time to locate John before he sailed.

'Would you ever be knowing the whereabouts of a fella called John Cattell darlin'?' Paddy asked the barmaid at *The Crown.*

'No I don't I'm sorry to say. But if you want to tell me all about him I'm willin' to listen.' She winked at Paddy, who blushed mildly, but enjoyed the flattery.

'He was 'ere but he's gone now,' declared a voice which emanated from an entity perched on the stool beside Paddy.

It was Ellen's brother in his usual position at the bar. His voice was hoarse and hardly audible. Years of dwelling in the bar enveloped by a grey haze, had seemingly smoked him like a kipper.

Paddy was visibly stung by this revelation. 'Then can you tell me where he's after goin'?'

'All's I know is he's got a ticket to America. He showed it to the landlord the day he left. He'll be sailin' on *The Liverpool Lady.'*

'Is it a friend of his you are?' Paddy enquired downing a hard-earned pint of warm beer.

'No, but me sister took a fancy to 'im once. Then he took off, disappeared like, broke 'er heart. A troubled man, very troubled, dying wife, three littluns.'

'Sure I know all about that my friend.'

'The name's Jacob.' He held out a crusty nicotine tarred hand, which Paddy gripped firmly.

'Good man Jacob. They call me Paddy McGuire. I'll be on my way home to my girls now, so I will.'

'Hope to see you again Paddy McGuire. They call me Ethel,' the barmaid declared.

'Pleased to meet you Ethel, I may well return. That was a grand pint.'

He set off to deliver the bad news to Bernie and

Colleen. He had been hopeful of an encounter with John, but in spite of his disappointment, the encounter with Ethel had lifted his flagging spirit. Her smile, like the sudden appearance of the sun from behind a mass of dark cloud, had penetrated the invisible fog of worry and anxiety accumulated over years of struggle and grief through which he fought to stay strong and cheerful. They had connected in an instant, and Paddy sensed a shift in his life's direction, feeling sure that Ethel would play a significant role in his future life. It was time to move on from his wife Kathleen's death; it's what she would have wanted.

On his arrival home Bernie and Colleen were perplexed by his cheerfulness as he announced his failure to find Catherine's father.

'He's on his way for sure,' he pronounced. 'And good riddance! A man who'd desert his wife and bairns that way has no claim on my heart. Let him rot in America.'

Early the following morning, as the weary sun struggled through an unyielding cloud laden winter dawn, *The Liverpool Lady* set sail for New York.

PART 2

LIVERPOOL 1890

Chapter 23

Funerals and Feathers

The day had not begun well, with ten funeral hats to complete and no black feathers, in spite of the order having been placed weeks earlier.

Catherine's fingers ached after a particularly busy week. All the ladies in Liverpool seemed to be dressing for occasions. Summer was always hectic, with garden fêtes and the races. Floral fashion filled the shop with vibrant colours, but this week had been devoted mostly to funeral hats; black lace and feathers to offset black felt, wide brims.

Consumption and cholera were taking their toll on the population of Liverpool, and sad funeral processions were a constant sight along Church St as they made their way to Saint Peter's for burial. If they were wealthy they would have a family grave with a headstone to commemorate their existence, whereas the poor would be lowered into an un-marked pauper's grave, where future generations would stand and wonder at the tragedy of that fate.

Through the constant stitching, Catherine was reminded of her oakum picking days at the workhouse, when her fingers became calloused, and although life had improved somewhat, there was still the daily grind to get through.

Living above the shop on Church St, in her own room with her own bed, was a great improvement compared to the six-to-a-bed days in the cold dormitory where she had jostled for space with Bernadette and Colleen, although her room was not much bigger than a coffin, it had a set of drawers for her few belongings and a window overlooking Church St, where she could spend candle-lit evenings watching.

The funeral was going to be a big one. Consumption had taken the daughter of one of the wealthy merchants

'It's not picky!' Molly, the shop owner had commented, as they laboured to finish the order. 'Consumption will carry off king and pauper.'

Catherine knew all about the merciless disease, and as Molly chattered on, her thoughts drifted to their house on Great Newton St, her mother's death and her father's disappearance. The terrible loss which had led to Aunt Lizzie leaving Catherine and her brothers in the workhouse.

'That's twenty finished with ten more to do, but the dark's setting in so we can't do any more. Cathy! Dreaming again! Did you hear a word I said?'

Catherine returned to the feather strewn shop and Molly's good-humoured smile.

'It's time to stop,' Molly mouthed with slow emphasis. 'Put down your needle. We have an early start tomorrow, so it's a quick supper and bed for us.'

Although it was late, a midsummer's glow lingered in the sky above Church St and, work weary Catherine knelt on the window seat watching the darkening figures of the street; theatre goers, horse drawn carriages, children, barefoot and ragged, yapping dogs, street sellers, seagulls, youths and young girls, penny whistlers and organ grinders, but Catherine's gaze was drawn to the children and she remembered. She was always remembering, always, always remembering when night after night she had wandered the streets and bars looking for their daddy; and here she was at the window still watching for him. She imagined that one day he would emerge from the alleyway opposite the hat shop like he had never been gone. Wearing his flat cap and loose white shirt, with the breeches he worn each day for work. He would be just as she remembered him before her mammy's sickness and she would run to his arms and all would be well.

The early dawn awakened her with little more than feathers on her mind and ten more hats to make. Molly was already in the workroom when Catherine arrived, still drowsy and not quite ready for the demands of the day.

'Get your porridge Cathy girl it's waitin' in the kitchen.' Molly ordered. 'We've the day from hell to get through!'

Molly approached each morning in this manner. Every

day was the one from hell, understandably so with the workload each new dawn brought. Sometimes it seemed they were making hats for all the women in Liverpool with only a week to complete the job.

In the tiny kitchen, Catherine began to wake up. Molly's porridge was far better than workhouse porridge; hot and creamy. Outside, the day was getting underway. Trams and carriages jostled for space and bleary eyed young clerks made their way to busy offices, shops put their shutters up and pulled bright awnings down, while the bells of Saint Peter's church announced the break of a new day.

In the busy workshop, unadorned hats were piled according to size and shape on shelves along the wall facing the entrance to the shop. A long pine table used up most of the space in the room, and to the left of the door stood three tall chests of drawers in which were kept trinkets used to decorate hats. The contents of these drawers, lace and ribbons of every colour imaginable, studs and sequins, feathers and bows, fascinated Catherine; a treasury of possibilities and Molly Briers had a talent for creating hats of style, so popular that she had a waiting list. She was an artist in her craft and never disappointed her faithful customers - from the young and fashionable who liked their hats to perch atop their head and piled high with lace, feathers, birds, butterflies or jewels, to the planer bonnets mostly the choice of the older lady, less ornate and often with a floral theme to brighten them.

Catherine spent most of her time in the workroom while Molly dealt with customers in the shop, which was always stocked with a variety of hats for men, women and children. When there were no orders to complete, Catherine would work on bonnets or picture hats for general stock.

'There's never an end in sight!' she would complain to Molly, who joined her whenever she was able to help with the stitching.

'The day there's an end in sight, will be the day my business dies young lady,' she would retort.

Molly was a friend of Miss Clancy, Catherine's sewing teacher at the workhouse. Miss Clancy had recommended Catherine as a good worker and seamstress, and Molly had no regrets about her decision to employ the pale-faced young girl who seldom smiled and seemed to carry the sorrows of the world on her shoulders, but her work could not be faulted.

'We need those black feathers Cathy, and there's no sign of the order arriving, so you'll have to pop round to Mrs. Sanders on Paradise St. I'll give you a note and some cash. Let's hope she has a few to spare. I've helped her out a few times. Here, wear this fancy bonnet and if anyone comments tell them who made it.'

Catherine gladly donned the daisy dressed bonnet and set off on the short trip to Paradise St. Early morning trams and carriages bringing workers into the city jostled for space along the road, leaving very little room for the wary pedestrians. The day promised to be a hot one, and the enticing aroma of freshly baked bread and coffee as she past Cooper's store, together with an earthy scent of horses and dust from sun dried streets, seagulls calling and the peel of bells from St Peter's Church, lifted her spirits. After hours of close work in the back room of Molly's shop, it was good to be outside.

She hurried towards Lord St, passing young flower girls and fruit stall owners arranging their bright fresh wares, relishing the sights and the brief spell of freedom. But the freedom was bittersweet and her mood darkened briefly at the thought of Alfie, her little brother, not yet free.

Mrs. Sanders was very obliging and supplied the required black feathers without hesitation. 'Lovely bonnet you're wearing! One of Molly's I take it? She's a talented lady,' Mrs. Sanders gushed.

'Thank you.' Catherine smiled and blushed, unaccustomed to compliments. 'We have a big funeral order to finish today,' she offered, feeling an explanation was required. 'The feathers didn't arrive in the post on time.'

'You can never rely on the post,' Mrs. Sanders sighed. 'Best be on your way and get to work young lady.'

Catherine thanked the elegant Mrs. Sanders and hastened back to Molly's. As she reached Church St she heard her name from somewhere above.

'Cathy! Catherine! It's me! On the tram!'

Looking up to the open top of the passing tram, she saw her cousin Maude waving vigorously.

'Maude! Where are you going?'

'I'm going to work, I'll call in at Molly's later tonight.'

Maude yelled as the tram jostled away up the now chaotic street. Catherine waved, brightened further by the encounter with her cousin Maude who doubled as her best friends.

'I love your bonnet!' Maude bellowed, pointing to her head just in case Catherine was out of earshot.

Chapter 24

The Storm

Liverpool was having a turbulent year. In March the dockworkers' union called a strike for more pay. Men travelled to Liverpool from other cities looking for work and hundreds found themselves stranded with no money to fund a journey home or to buy food and drink. They were directed to the workhouse. Their desperation forced hundreds to endure the shame with no other choice but starvation. The rules forbade them to stay for only a day, in order to be nourished. If they were admitted they must stay at least a week and work. Many of the stranded refused, but others could find no alternative and the Liverpool workhouse, already an overcrowded mire of misery, became home to the broken strikers. Their fury potent and intimidating.

'Keep out their way Alf,' Billy urged his little brother. 'I don't like the look of any of them.'

The brothers were together in the dining hall, two bags of bones among row upon row of the same.

'Whatever you do don't look at them,' Billy reiterated.

Alfie was ten years old, a slight, fair haired boy with bright blue eyes. 'Don't worry Bill. I can look after meself,' he whispered.

Billy was worried. He would be leaving Alfie for the day to work on *The Coral*, Captain Featherstone's boat, which would be sailing to the Isle of Man with him on board. Soon he would be going on long voyages and have no need to stay at the workhouse, but the captain had arranged for day release permission while he learned the ropes. There was often tension and aggression in the male quarters of the workhouse, but now there was tangible resentment between the Liverpool and Manchester inmates, which Billy sensed could lead to violence.

Breakfast over, they filed out and Bill tousled his little brother's hair. 'Keep clear of trouble. I'll see you later.'

Alf playfully punched his brother in the stomach and they parted, grinning.

Alfie spent mornings in the school room. He set off across the yard with his group of friends.

'Billy said to keep away from the new dockers he advised them. 'They're bad and angry.'

'Not happy that's for sure,' Alex agreed. Alex was the son of a Russian migrant, a skilled engineer, trying to find his way in the city, but now dependent on the workhouse for survival. Alf and Alex had become good friends since the latter's arrival in February. Both boys were survivors in the classroom in spite of the strict supervision and punishment for the slightest misdemeanour.

Beyond the rooftops and chimney stacks above them, a patch of blue sky hung feebly overhead, while dark storm clouds edged in, and shadows loomed. Alfie saw a seagull streak across the cloud, its whiteness captured by a single ray of disappearing sun, and for a moment thought about beyond the walls, to where the River Mersey lay and Billy sailing on the boat to Isle of Man.

~

The funeral hat order complete, Catherine tidied the workshop and studied the orders for the next batch, which were mostly lavish picture hats, her favourite. Molly would design them according to the customer's request regarding colour and ornamentation, and would instruct Catherine on the making. The hat trade had suffered due to the introduction of factories, which could turn out many more hats in a day than Molly and Catherine were able to manage in a month, but it was Molly's personal touch that kept her business buoyant. Molly Briar's hats were gaining fame amongst the ladies of Liverpool.

'Right Cathy we need blue net, feathers, birds and ribbon out on the table to start with. Here's the base. Now that hat is for Mrs. Bagshaw, a good customer and very influential, so I need top notch work from you.'

Catherine nodded nervously, it seems a huge responsibility.

'Don't worry, I'll guide you every step of the way,' Molly smiled. 'Get everything on the table and ready to go!'

The rest of the day was devoted to Mrs. Bagshaw's blue hat and Catherine was so absorbed she hardly noticed the violent thunderstorm that raged outside, until Molly called her to help sweep the rain water away from the shop, by which time the worst had passed and only a steady patter remained, as rain drenched Church St gleamed clean and freshly polished by the downpour. The two fought gallantly against the sudden torrent, which had rushed along Bold St and Church St, joining in with the laughter of shoppers and shopkeepers caught out by the storm, which was slowly moving out to the Irish Sea.

The shop was spared and, still giggling from the drama, Molly put the kettle on the stove. 'We deserve a cup of tea Cathy my dear!'

The two settled by the stove in the cosy kitchen, removing their shoes to dry them in the warmth.

'What'll you do on your day off tomorrow Cathy?' Molly asked, watching her little helper, who at fourteen years of age could pass for twelve.

Scrawny was the word used by Mrs. Bagshaw; 'You're telling me that that scrawny little waif is working on my hat?' She had whined when Molly mentioned that Catherine was busy stitching the blue symphony together.

'She is a very proficient needle-worker Mrs. Bagshaw, I can assure you utmost satisfaction.' Molly had gushed, secretly hoping that the "little waif" would not let her down.

'I'll call on Auntie Lizzie,' Catherine responded, enjoying the rare break and hot drink. 'I saw Maude on the tram this mornin' she was shoutin' and wavin' from the top deck, Cathy, Cathy!' she parodied Maude's behaviour and the two laughed again. 'She said she was going to call in later, but she was on her way to work so I don't know when she'll finish.'

'Maude's working?' Mollie queried. She had met Catherine's cousin a few times now and understood the close friendship shared by the two cousins. 'What's she doing?'

'I don't know Molly. It's the first I've heard of it.'

'Oh well, all will be revealed soon enough no doubt.

Now back to that hat with you. We have another hour of daylight before supper.'

Chapter 25

A Tragedy at Sea

When Billy arrived at *The Coral,* the crew were stowing cargo. Captain Featherstone greeted him and set him to work on the rigging. The River Mersey was as busy as ever, with ships in dock, ferries crossing to the Wirral, and smaller sailing boats bobbing on the water here and there. Out at sea the waves were restless, but that was not unusual on the Irish Sea, and the Captain anticipated an uneventful crossing with time for lunch at the Isle of Man, returning to Liverpool early evening.

Within an hour of reaching open seas a thin haze began to mask the sun, like a bride's veil, and before long they watched the storm explode above Liverpool; lightning relentlessly stabbing at the city, thunder rattling long and loud and as they watched, the dense, murky storm cloud shifted ominously in their direction.

'We're afore storm lads,' the Captain called. 'It's slow moving, so let's get ready for battle!'

Billy had never experienced a storm at sea, but trusted his captain to get them through. He followed the rest of the crew in securing cargo and battening down the hatches, but he sensed the severity of the approaching onslaught.

~

As Billy prepared to face the biggest battle of his life, Catherine battled with the yards of blue net on Mrs. Bagshaw's hat, and Alfie battled with his six-times tables in the workhouse classroom.

By suppertime Maude had not arrived, and though

Catherine watched from her window she knew, as darkness fell, that Auntie Lizzie would not allow her cousin to wander the streets. She glanced across to the alleyway from whence her father would one day emerge, or so she yearned and accepted that her curiosity would have to wait until her visit to Great Newton St tomorrow, when Maude would tell her about her new employment, and she would tell her cousin about Mrs. Bagshaw's blue hat. Then in her darkened room and listening to the sounds of Church St night life, while a glow from the street lamps peeped through the curtains casting narrow shafts of light upon her bedroom walls, she thought with an aching heart about her daddy and brothers and prayed they would be safe.

Chapter 26

A Surprise Encounter

Maude had found employment with a family living in an opulent house on the outskirts of the city. Events had unfolded so quickly she had no time to tell Catherine about her new status. Their grandmother Margaret, had noticed the advertisement in the *Echo* - Liverpool's local newspaper - and suggested to Maude that she apply. Within days of sending her letter, the lady of the house, Mrs. Bagshaw, had called to see Maude, astonishing the family with her huge, purple taffeta presence, which filled their tiny parlour.

'A remarkably clean room,' she approved, 'and Maude, my first impression of you is that you are a sensible, comely girl. I would like to trial you for three weeks. If all is well you will have a permanent place in my household. You must be prompt and keep my house as spick as this room. Come tomorrow morning at seven o'clock. There is a tram that leaves Lime St at half past six. Alight at the Newsham stop and there will be a woman by the name of Edith awaiting your arrival. If you miss the tram, do not bother coming. Good day to you all.' Whereupon, Mrs. Bagshaw emptied the room of her presence and returned to her carriage, leaving Maude and her family dumbstruck.

It was the following morning that Maude spotted her cousin Catherine from the tram and promised to call on her later to give her the news, but on her return at eight o'clock that evening, she was too weary for social calls and chose instead to go straight home. Neither girl could have predicted the circumstances of their next meeting.

Chapter 27

The Long Wait

Catherine was awakened by the shop bell jangling and loud banging on the door.

'Dear God it's morning already!' she cried, jumping out of bed and hastily pulling on her skirt and blouse. The knocking continued, and a dazed Molly met her at the top of the stairs.

'What in the name of all that's holy is happening?'

They sped down the stairs, through the workshop to the front door, where through the frosted glass they could perceive two figures.

'Who's there?' called Molly, nervously, wondering what could be the cause of this commotion.

'It's us Molly; Denis and Maude. We need to talk to Catherine.'

Without hesitation, Molly unlocked the door and opened it to find father and daughter, extremely disturbed and anxious on her doorstep.

'Come in won't you? It's an unearthly time to be callin' round mind. What's happened?' she asked, ushering them inside. Denis set his lamp down on the kitchen table and Maude took Catherine in her arms.

'There's been a storm over the Irish Sea Cathy.' Denis was panting after rushing through the streets.

'The same storm that almost flooded us out, no doubt.' Molly added.

'The very one,' Denis nodded solemnly.

Catherine had stiffened in Maude's grasp and had already guessed what she was about to hear. 'No!' she cried.

'No, don't say it! I won't hear it! I won't hear it! Not Billy!'

Molly, now fully awake became alert to the situation. 'What happened?' she asked.

'Some boats went down in the storm. *The Coral* hasn't been seen since. Some were saved and some are dead. Billy hasn't been found.' Denis could hardly contain his emotions, while recounting what he knew of the tragedy.

'Not found?' Catherine murmured. 'Not found is hopeful Uncle Denis. Don't you think Maude? It's hopeful. We'll wait, and soon we'll hear that he's alive. Our Billy's strong and would never break our hearts.'

Molly was stoking the stove, aware that Catherine may not be able to bear the loss of her brother. 'What can we do Denis?' she asked, bringing calm to the room.

'We must go to the Pier Head,' Catherine responded. 'We must go and wait for our Billy to come home.'

Chapter 28

The River Vigil

At the Pier Head, a subdued gathering kept vigil at the water's edge, as the river gently lapped the landing stage and a full moon brightened foamy waves. Waiting people stood motionless, listening and watching for a single sign of life on the bleak horizon. Boats arrived at intervals, bringing the living and the dead ashore. Scenes of joy and grief unfolded where only hours before the unsuspecting sailors had embarked upon their journeys.

The four stood in hope of Billy's return. They spoke not a word, but stared into the dark abyss that was the Irish Sea, willing Billy alive. As she waited, unaware that in the shadows another anxious figure stood close by, Catherine thought about her mammy sailing in from Ireland to seek refuge from the terrible famine. As a little girl, her mammy had stepped safely from the boat.

'If only Billy would do the same,' she thought. 'Bring him home mammy, bring him home.' But the darkness was intense.

Inevitably, dawn began to break, pink clouds and seagulls hailed another day and a voice called out: 'There's another boat coming!' And there, on the pale horizon, could be seen the sails, bright in the new dawn, of a small craft.

'It may be *The Coral*.'

A murmur rippled along the quayside while an old sailor pulled a telescope from the pocket of his coat and peered out to where the boat was gliding closer and closer to the cold and weary hopefuls. Molly and Maude drew nearer to Catherine. All eyes were fixed on the sea weathered old man with his telescope.

'It's *The Coral* all right,' he finally announced, and Catherine's legs buckled. Molly and Maude were ready with support. The people remained quiet and soon *The Coral* could be clearly seen by all.

Chapter 29

A Brother Alone

Alfie lay awake in the bed he shared with four other boys of varying age and size. Billy had not returned in time and had been locked out of the workhouse for the night. There was no way to find out what had happened to him, and Alfie wondered where he would be and whether or not he was safe. The streets of Liverpool were dangerous at night. He began to fear the day ahead and what terrible news it might bring. What if he never came back? How would he manage without Billy?

Daylight slowly seeped into the dismal room, there was a strong odour of urine, bed-wetting being an unfortunate and frequent occurrence among the younger boys. Alfie watched the slumbering men and boys, remembering Billy's warning. There had been some tension throughout the previous day and a number of inmates had been expelled from the place. The morning bell rang and reluctantly, a mass of bony arms and legs began to stir.

Chapter 30

Joy and Despair

'Jaysus Cathy we heard the news and ran straight here. They say *The Coral*'s missin' and I know Billy's on it.'

Colleen enveloped Catherine with a comforting hug. She had arrived at the riverside with Bernadette and Paddy, sick with worry for her Billy, but working hard to conceal the depth of her feelings. The three were breathless from the rush to be with their friends.

The sky had changed from pink to powder blue, dappled with puffs of white cloud drifting above *The Coral*, escorting her home.

'*The Coral*'s coming in Paddy, but I won't rejoice until I see Billy in the flesh,' Denis uttered, cautious and practical, as was his nature. Molly shivered in the early morning chill. They had been standing for hours, so mesmerised by the moonlit silent vigil that they hardly noticed the creeping cold which gripped their bones.

The Coral reached the quayside and thick, heavy ropes were thrown ashore. Catherine saw them and for an involuntary moment was back at the workhouse picking oakum, tearing those thick ropes apart, trapped and hopeless, but now she would trade a lifetime of the same for her brother to be safe.

The crew was silent as they moored the boat and lowered the ramp, then with quiet dignity, two men bore a stretcher to land and placed it on the ground. The crowd remained restrained as one by one the sailors came ashore. Then Billy, subdued and bereft of his usual zeal, appeared and was engulfed by fourteen relieved and loving arms, which ushered him swiftly away from the scene and all that he could utter were the awful words; 'The Captain's dead.'

The riverside remained a scene of quiet joy and devastating grief, while sunbeams began to warm the day and the dark drama of that night was dispersed by seagull cries and sparkling waves.

A lone figure rested on a rusty bollard. Since the storm had drifted out to sea, John Cattell had waited for *The Coral* to return, had watched as boats sailed in and brought the bodies back throughout the night, had watched his anguished daughter and wanted to be with her, as he knew he should, but now was not the time. For now, he knew that Billy was safe. For now, that was enough.

Chapter 31

Mr. Cranny

At breakfast there was still no news of Billy, and Alfie was shocked when the prayer reader, charged with the duty of reading Bible extracts and praying for those who partook in the meagre morsel that was breakfast, mentioned the souls of those who had perished in the Irish Sea last night.

'It von't be Billy Alf. I pvomees you!' Alex had comforted in his deep, Russian cadence. 'I zink zay tell you eef it is Bill.'

'I hope you're right Alex.'

'Vee must vait and hope.'

The school room was hot and Mr. Cranny paced the creaky floorboards while the boys laboured to emulate the copperplate script displayed on the chalk-board. Alfie excelled at this, but Alex's effort lacked any resemblance to the original and Mr. Cranny struck him with his cane.

'Useless boy! You call this handwriting? A monkey could do better!' he bellowed.

The blow was unexpected and Alex's face reddened with anger and fear.

'Do it again and keep to the lines!' Mr. Cranny roared.
Luckily the bell heralded end of school and the boys filed out in perfect silence.

'Von day I vill murder Cranny,' Alex muttered.

'Soon I hope,' Alfie responded placing a hand on his friend's shoulder as they made their way across the yard to join the queue for lunch before their work routines began.

'Where's your Billy, Alf?' queried a tall, gaunt boy, one of Billy's gang.

'I don't know George. He never came back yesterday. He went out on *The Coral* to the Isle of Man. I hope he's alright.'

'*The Coral* came back Alf. Captain dead but crew survived. Jack the warden was talking about it. Bill should be back soon.'

Alfie and Alex exchanged rare gleeful glances. It was the best news Alf had ever received in his short lifetime.

Chapter 32

The Thankful

'You'd best come back with me Billy lad.' Denis lay a sympathetic hand on his nephew's shoulder.

Billy shrugged it off. 'No thanks Uncle Denis, I'll be fine.' In his despair he could not forget that had it not been for, what he considered, the heartlessness of his Uncle Denis and Aunty Lizzie, he and his brother and sister would not have been forced to suffer life in the workhouse. And although at heart he knew his father was to blame, he could not easily forgive the pair whose decision it had been to let them go.

Catherine shared his anger, but her friendship with Maude gave her a different perspective. She understood the desperation that had pushed Aunt Lizzie to act the way she had.

'Sure, he can stay with us Den,' Paddy offered swiftly, expelling the uncomfortable moment. It was agreed by all that this was a good solution, since Molly had nowhere for Billy to sleep, and quietly wished to restore normal routine to her life as soon as possible.

Scotland Rd was already buzzing with life when Paddy, Colleen, Billy and Bernie arrived exhausted from anxiety and lack of sleep. Forlorn children huddled on doorsteps, housewives shook dust from tattered rugs. The stench of beer and urine hung in the air from Saturday night pub revellers, and feral dogs rested as the sun began to warm the day. Paddy and his daughters shared a large room on the ground floor of a three-storey terraced house, the numerous inhabitants of which would have populated a small village in rural England.

Their room was neat and pleasant, benefiting from Bernie and Colleen's homely touch and their father Paddy's meagre but regular income from his work on the railway. There were chairs to sit on and a bed each, as well as a table to eat at and a stove. Compared to the workhouse life, they were living in luxury.

Colleen warmed a pan of porridge as daylight brightened the room. Billy had a long tale to tell of his survival through the storm, but it could wait. Sleep beckoned, and they gladly responded. Paddy drew the blinds and gave Billy half of his bed. They slept the sleep of the thankful.

It was the break of a solemn day in Liverpool and the bells of St Peter's sounded a mournful note in respect for those who had died at sea.

KNOWLE 1890

Chapter 33

A Big Decision

At her bakery in Knowle, Mary Cattell sat down for a break with her daughter Kate. They had been busy making pastry and dough for the morning rush and would soon leave the work for Mary's son Tom to complete overnight.

'It's been too long with no word Kate and you know how I worry. It's starting to get me down love,' Mary fretted.

'You know John mother, he doesn't think. Gets wrapped up in his problems and the world can go hang itself. He'll be fine, back with his children safe and sound,' Kate comforted.

It had been six months since John Cattell left the pretty village of his birth to return to the colossus of a city that Liverpool had become. Mary and the family had helped him through the crisis he endured after Ann Marie's death, and on his return he had been strong and confident that he would be reunited with his children. Mary waited for word from him, but as time passed began to despair.

'It's a rum place that Liverpool. The stories I hear! He might have been press-ganged and forced to slave on a ship all over the place, or gone on a prison ship to Australia. There are people would kill for a slice of bread, Kate.' She sipped her tea. Her round face pale with a dusting of flour, always present after a baking session.

'Mother! John can take care of himself,' Kate scolded, feeling impatient with her older brother whose self-pitying approach to life was beyond her comprehension. 'He has a good skill and three children to look after. He'll be too busy to write to us.'

'I feel I must go Kate.' Mary had made up her mind.

'What nonsense! You in Liverpool? You'll be gobbled up mother. They're hard, hungry folk and I'm not letting you go. That's final.' Kate was furious at the notion.

The sun was setting to the sound of birdsong through an open window. At their solid wooden table, the two women drank tea in silence, contemplating. Mary had hardly ever strayed beyond the boundaries of Knowle, let alone travel the long road to Liverpool. She surveyed her life; the sacks of flour, trays of dough, jars of sugar and spice, the fragrance of baking. It would be hard to leave, yet leave she must.

Chapter 34

Mr. Dooley

Since John had lingered on the quayside watching the America bound ship, *The Liverpool Lady*, gently drift towards the horizon, hopeful passengers waving their final farewells to the Motherland, he had experienced a terrible regret, and yet was sure he had made the right choice. There was no place for him, but here, with his children and soon it would be time to gather them together.

Since the ship sailed, he had found work with a small printing firm called Dooley's, which specialized in religious books. He enjoyed preparing the intricate lithographs of biblical characters and events. He knew his craft well and Mr. Dooley appreciated skill, paying him a fair price for each completed print.

'You've got talent John, and the best way to use it is in the service of the Lord,' Mr. Dooley would piously pronounce.

He was a kind man, with good intentions, which John appreciated, but piety was not a character trait which he could stomach in large doses. Fortunately his employer spent most of his time away from the premises doing good deeds for the downtrodden masses, as well as seeking outlets for his business amongst the new middle class church goers and clergy.

John's work was not motivated by religious fervour, but by his desire to put things right for his family. As he worked, he planned, and wondered what had become of the young lad to whom he had tossed his ticket to New York that misty February dawn, when he had forgone his journey in order to seek out his children. The ragged youth had not hesitated to take his ticket and board the ship, and John had wished him well as he sailed towards his new life.

Chapter 35

Changes

Life at the workhouse had been briefly brightened by Billy's return that Sunday evening, although his usual cheer was replaced by a solemn gravitas after the loss of his beloved captain, his friends were pleased to see him and Alfie was beside himself with joy.

'Don't leave me again Bill. I thought you weren't comin' back. Didn't know what to do. I was going to come lookin' for you.'

They were sitting on the cobbles in the grey yard, but Billy's thoughts were elsewhere, on *The Coral* battling the storm, the torrent of rain, wild wind, forks of lightning stabbing the restless waves and his captain falling. He shuddered at the memory. His captain was no more.

'I won't leave you Alf,' he promised. 'I won't leave you again.'

The solemn brothers remained together on the cobbles as the scarlet sun set.

Chapter 36

Careless Words

By Monday morning Molly and Catherine were back to work on a big order for the races. The hats were fun to make with lavish, colourful decorations; birds, butterflies and exotic feathers piled high on a straw plate with silk ribbons to tie in a huge bow beneath the chin.

The ladies of Liverpool were in high spirits when they came to try their special Molly creations, and Catherine's fingers ached from endless needle-work.

'I think we need help Cathy,' Molly announced late that evening. 'There's so much to do and I know you're working as fast as you can, but it's not enough. I'm going to ask Marion Clancy if she can send another worker. It means you'll have to share your room and bed, but you're used to that, coming from the workhouse.'

Catherine did not allow Molly to see how badly her words had hurt. She continued to stitch and kept her head bowed. Molly was a kind employer, but a business woman at heart, and her father had instilled in her the notion that there is no heart in business. She was a plain talker and it did not occur to her that she had been carelessly hurtful towards Catherine, but sadly, the words she had spoken unknowingly caused a rift which would never be mended.

Chapter 37

Weary Travellers

Mary and Kate arrived late and spent the night in a temperance hotel recommended by Mary's neighbour, Martha.

'Plain but clean,' Martha had pronounced as they sipped tea at Mary's baking table the evening before their departure. 'And no drunken sailors!'

Mary was relieved to know this, never having travelled far beyond Knowle. She had heard worrying stories about Liverpool, which made her flesh creep, but Martha was a decent soul and trustworthy.

The hotel was situated on Lord St, near the coach stop, and a willing young porter carried their luggage, which consisted of one ancient brown leather trunk, to the portal of The Oak Hotel. The journey had been long and the road between Knowle and Liverpool was far from smooth, leaving the two travellers weary and aching. Although it was late, laughter and music emanated from the numerous public houses close by, and cold, bedraggled children crouched beneath the gas lamps.

Mary and Kate hurried up the scrubbed steps of The Oak to be greeted by Mrs. Quayle, a stout lady from Drumour in the north of Ireland.

'It's yer beds that yer need'n afther such a long journey,' she cooed and gently guided them to their sparse, but clean and welcoming room. With great relief they locked the door and too exhausted for further dealing with that day, were soon slumbering soundly.

Chapter 38

New Girl

The new girl arrived a week after Molly's announcement. She was small with a mass of black curls and her name was Vera. Apart from the startling cloud of hair framing her anxious countenance, Vera was remarkable for her silence.

'She's never spoke a word Colleen,' Catherine told her friend, one warm and pleasant Sunday as they strolled from Church St to the workhouse. They longed to get word of Billy and Alf, neither of whom they had seen or heard from since the storm. Captain Featherstone was dead and Billy no longer had his sponsorship or the freedom he had enjoyed before the tragedy.

A host of seagulls swept the sky calling frantically as they dipped and dived, the fanfare for another splendid summer day. Both girls were wearing Molly's bonnets for the morning, adorned with daisies and roses, light cotton shawls draped around their shoulders, green for Catherine and Colleen's was pale blue to match the sky that day.

'Such pretty pictures,' Molly had gushed; she liked her hats to be worn around the town, and often picked up a few orders after such excursions atop Cathy's head.

'You were the same Cathy. Sure, remember how Bernie and I worried about you before we took you to see Alfie in the choir?' Colleen reminded her.

They met Maude on the way as they passed her house on Great Newton St and linked arms together, united as they approached the workhouse.

'It's not the place to be on a lovely day like today,' Colleen uttered, mournfully, remembering the dismal days of their confinement. The three were suddenly silent as the shadow of the monstrous edifice obscured the sun and made them shudder. Standing at the old familiar meeting gate, Catherine recalled the dread she had felt when Colleen and Bernie left the workhouse and she was alone.

They passed that gate and soon reached the main entrance which they decided would be more helpful for their quest.

'It's the girlies!' crowed a voice they all knew well, as they approached the gate. 'Cathy and Colleen look at you now, in yer flower 'ats. Are yer missin' us girlies? Want to come back?' The old woman cackled with benign pleasure, limping towards them with a wide, toothless grin.

'Gertie!' cried the girls genuinely happy to see one of the few sources of warmth beyond the gates.

'Ave you come to visit? I'm just on my way in' Gertie informed them as if inviting them for tea and cake in a salubrious pile somewhere far away from Brownlow Hill.

'Ach sure Gertie darlin' we're after lookin' for Billy and Alfie, Cathy's brothers. It's been a while since we had news of them so it has,' Colleen chirped.

'So you's 'aven't 'eard?' Gertie's sagging features darkened and Catherine's heart skipped a beat.

'Heard what Gertie?' she asked, turning cold with fear.

Gert was a drama queen and enjoyed being the bearer of tidings, whether good or bad.

'They've went,' she said peering steadily at Catherine with her cloudy eyes.

'Went where?' Colleen queried, 'and why have they went?'

Chapter 39

The Bluecoat School

The atmosphere in the men's block of the workhouse had resembled a restless volcano since the Manchester dock strikers had been admitted. Bill and his friends steered clear of the hostility. The Manchester men had journeyed to Liverpool to join the rally, which achieved nothing, and were now obliged to rely on the workhouse for food, an entitlement the more troublesome Liverpool inmates resented.

Due to the overcrowding many of the young boys including Bill, Alf and Alex were moved to the Bluecoat School, an establishment which, although also bursting at the seams, was solely for children and therefore a safer environment. The boys were grateful to have remained together, and Alfie was especially joyful to be singing in the choir at St Peter's Church on Church St, which traditionally enrolled children from the school. The move was so swift they had no way to relay the news to Catherine.

Chapter 40

Vera's Dilemma

It was a bright Monday morning when mother and daughter emerged from The Oak Hotel onto the sun-drenched streets of Liverpool. They were excited by the vibrancy of the city, and how purposeful the people were. There was a sense of optimism about the place where people gathered on their way to the New World. They saw the very rich and the very poor sharing the streets. Barefoot, raggedy children played on the steps of St George's Hall, a huge neo-classic pile designed to reflect the success of the great port. They dodged the horse-drawn trams and carriages along Church St, and were drawn by the rich aroma of coffee exuding from Cooper's, an elegant café and grocery store. Mary had dipped into her savings for the trip and felt that a breakfast at Cooper's would be a justifiable treat after their long journey the previous day.

'I don't feel dressed for it mother,' Kate protested somewhat mildly, '...but why not?' she giggled and entwined her arms with Mary's as they walked proudly into the oak panelled café, dazzled by the chandeliers and gleaming floor-to-ceiling mirrors. The tables were covered with white cotton, lace trimmed cloths and seated around them were the crème de la crème of Liverpool society, daintily sipping from delicate china cups. They were escorted to a window table from which they could watch the unfolding of the Liverpool morning.

'These people seem quite normal to me Kate,' Mary whispered conspiratorially. 'Nothing like the thieves and murderers I expected from what Martha was telling me. They're just going about their day.'

'Not one murder to be witnessed,' smiled Kate,

studying the menu. 'How disappointing!'

Mary ignored the sarcasm. 'Mind you, it wouldn't be happening in broad daylight. The nights will be different.'

Although their attire was plain compared to the lavish cut of the ladies at Cooper's, the two were smart in their fitted jackets, white lace-trimmed blouses, long skirts and polished leather shoes. Mary had insisted they look their best for finding John. Kate had chosen green taffeta and Mary, navy blue linen, and had the suits tailored especially for the trip. However, they were both aware that their outfits lacked something that seemed requisite for a lady to be truly acceptable in places such as Cooper's of Liverpool. They were in fact enthralled by the hats of so many colours and such variety of décor.

'I wouldn't want one that was too lavish,' Mary confided. 'Simple, but with a few of those feathers, a nice pale blue perhaps.'

'I fancy the white roses and possibly a butterfly,' said Kate, beginning to feel excited at the prospect of owning one of the works of art sported by the women out and about this summer morning.

They had walked for only a minute after leaving Cooper's, when they came across the shop: Molly's Hats.

'Let's go inside for a look,' said Mary.

Molly was busy dusting off some pretty, floral hat boxes, popular with the spring hat customers, when Mary and Kate arrived at her shop. Vera was in the back room stitching scarlet feathers onto a wide brimmed black hat, destined for the lead actress in a play showing at the Empire theatre.

'Good morning ladies, how may I help you?' Molly enquired, sliding the boxes aside.

'Good morning. We are hoping to purchase hats and would like to view a few bonnets and plate style,' Kate said, already eyeing some generously decorated creations displayed on a variety of dummy heads around the shop.

After some serious discourse and deliberation, choices were made which required a few adjustments of décor and colour.

'We only have the week here in Liverpool,' said Mary, and would appreciate your haste in preparing out hats.'

'They will be ready for collection tomorrow, madam,

rest assured. Your good name please?' Molly enquired, pen hovering over the receipt.

'Mrs. Mary Cattell', replied Mary, spelling it out for Molly, who registered, with some surprise, the fact that these seemingly well-to-do ladies shared the same unusual surname as Catherine, but felt it of no consequence and had no intention of trying to link her customers with the little workhouse refugee who was presently out visiting her brothers at the Bluecoat Chambers for destitute children.

As the two Cattells left the shop, Molly shrugged off thoughts of any connections and resumed her task of dusting hat boxes.

Vera, however, felt otherwise. She had been listening to the conversation and on hearing the name given by the elderly, white-haired woman, she put down her work and waited for Molly to comment on the coincidence, surprised that she had allowed the pair to leave without a word about Catherine. Having witnessed Catherine's pain each night as she waited at the window for her daddy, there was no greater desire in Vera's life than to see her workmate happily united with her family.

If she could only break free from her silent state, she would let Catherine know what had happened on her return, but her voice had withered over years of disuse and she no longer had the skill to make the sounds or form the words that those around her longed to hear. Her doleful, deep blue eyes had seen such horrors and her body subjected to such pain and neglect, before the age that language should begin to flow. It never flowed from Vera. Locked within her silent world, she had been raised in the workhouse from the age of three.

Chapter 41

A Clue

'My feet have never been so sore!' said Mary, perched on her bed in their tidy room back at the hotel, rubbing her swollen ankles.' We must have traipsed for miles today and all for nothing.'

'I wouldn't say for nothing, mother,' Kate responded, endeavouring to erase the failures of their day. 'At least we know where John isn't, and we have our hats to collect in the morning.'

'I'd rather be collecting John tomorrow, Kate.'

The two had walked to Brownlow Hill and sought John's old address, now occupied by an Irish couple and their large brood.

'We'v bin 'ere a year ma luvs,' the weary woman told them in a quiet Irish lilt. 'Sure we don't be knowin' a John Cattell.'

Disappointed, the women made their way down the cobbled hill and back to the town centre.

'What's that awful place, I wonder?' Said Kate, looking back over her shoulder at the vast, Gothic building, blocking out the sunlight.'

'Some sort of prison, mayhap,' Mary mused. 'I think it may be the workhouse. I feel sorry for any poor soul that finds themselves in there.'

Kate shuddered.

'What next, I wonder?' Mary could not conceive of a way to find her son in this great, busy city teeming with people, trams, carriages, dogs, cats, pigeons and seagulls. Where could John be amongst it all?

A leather bound Bible lay on the mahogany bedside table between the two narrow beds. Mary, rested her tired body, propped up by two generously feathered pillows and for want of something to do, reached for it and began to turn the pages, her thoughts in turmoil. She knew her Bible well and was comforted by the familiar presentation of verse and chapter, and admired the intricate illuminated lettering which prefaced each chapter. Soon she was engrossed and silent as Kate dozed, an ornate clock sitting proudly on the polished surface of a tall dark oak dresser, ticked loudly and outside there was chatter and the clip clopping of horses hooves as the populace went about their business.

'I think I've found him Kate,' she suddenly murmured, staring at the book in her hands. Kate stirred from her slumber.

'I didn't know you'd lost him mother, you always seemed so strong in your faith.' Kate looked sincerely concerned.

'I don't mean I've found God, Kate! I've found John! Come and look at this.'

Kate agreed that the signature on a print depicting the Angel Gabriel in the preface to the New Testament, was John's: 'I'd know it anywhere Kate. He practised it so much when he was a lad. Look, Benjamin Dooley, Printer, Lord St, Liverpool. Seems our plan for tomorrow is sorted.'

Chapter 42

The Print Works

The next morning displayed another clear blue sky for the residents of Liverpool to enjoy. Benjamin Dooley was early as usual at his small print works, pondering the fact that his lithographer, John Cattell, had not been to work for three days. It was common for him to stay away for a day or two, after which he would arrive with sketches and ideas for the work in progress, a prayer book for children, which would be well received by the well-to-do Liverpool church goers. John's prints were fashionably detailed and sentimental. Three more illustrations were required before the book could go to print and Mr. Dooley hoped that would be soon in order to boost his dwindling coffers. However, a three day absence with no explanation was more than he was happy to accept, and although John had been his employee for almost a year, he had no idea where he lived or if he had family thereabouts. There was little hope of finding a replacement with John's talent and consequently, he may be forced to publish *The Little Cherub's Prayer Book*, minus three illustrations.

So deep were his thoughts that he failed to notice the entrance of two comely ladies who now stood before him in his small, dusty office, littered with inks and stencils and shelves lined with ornately scribed religious publications.

Chapter 43

Vera's Anguish

Catherine was subdued on her return from visiting Billy and Alfie at the Bluecoat Chambers, conscious that their confinement remained indefinite. Since Captain Featherstone's death, Billy had failed to find a sponsor and seemed to have lost his enthusiasm for the sea. 'It's better than the workhouse here, an' Alfie's still in the choir,' he told his sister. 'But it's time we had a home again Cathy.'

She couldn't get his words out of her mind and felt that all her hopes of getting the family together again were fading.

Vera was waiting and hoping that Molly would mention the two women who had been in the shop that day to Catherine. However, at supper, Molly talked about everything but their visit.

'We need to bring the black and scarlet ware down from the top shelf Catherine. You'll be working on a fancy piece for a new customer tomorrow. She sent her maid along with a sketch and will be coming in to the shop in a day or two. Vera, you have a few orders to finish off tomorrow. The daisy bonnets are doing well lately, which reminds me Catherine, I'll need you to call on Mrs. Sanders, she's got a surplus of daisies and we could do with some extras.'

The young girls listened attentively to Molly. They worked long hours, especially now the days were lengthening as summer unfurled, but Molly was a kind employer and the hats they worked on were such delightful creations that neither girl felt bitter about her lot, especially since both had experienced the workhouse regime.

Catherine and Molly accepted Vera's silence and no

longer expected her to respond verbally. She communicated through gesture and expression, and her needlework could not be faulted.

At bedtime that night Catherine was aware that Vera seemed restless and agitated.

'Is something wrong?' she asked, taking her usual position at the window and checking the street beyond. 'I know you think I'm mad, Vera, lookin' for me dad every night, but I don't think I'll ever stop. Not until me dyin' day.'

Chapter 44

Finding John

'Good morning ladies. Benjamin Dooley at your service, how can I help you?' Mr. Dooley buttoned his overcoat and checked the silver fob watch hanging from the pocket of his brown, pin-striped waistcoat, for no particular reason but to look busy and important.

'Straight to the point Mr. Dooley', Mary announced locking eyes with the large gentleman who seemed to fill the space behind the counter. 'We're here in search of my son, John Cattell.'

'Indeed? In that case dear ladies, please let me know when you find him.'

Kate and Mary exchanged disappointed glances. 'You mean he's not here?' Kate responded, putting a comforting arm around her mother.

'No sign of John for three days and I'm waiting for some work from him.' Mr. Dooley sighed.

'Ohh Kate!' Mary wailed. 'I thought we'd found him.' 'Mother!' Kate's arms were around Mary guiding her towards a chair beside the counter. 'What are we going to do Kate? Where can we look now?'

Ben Dooley was shocked at the poor woman's distress and regretted his abrupt response.

'Dear, dear madam. I apologise. How could I be so heartless? May God forgive me? It's not unusual for John to disappear for a few days. I dare say he'll be here before the weekend. No need to despair.'

Mary took some comfort from the words and Kate cast an appreciative glance towards Mr. Dooley. 'We've come all the way from Knowle looking for John, Mr. Dooley. Haven't seen or heard from him for such a long time,' Kate explained. 'There's a Bible in our lodgings with one of his prints inside. Mother recognized his signature. We thought we'd find him here, so you can appreciate our disappointment, I hope.'

Mr. Dooley listened sympathetically. 'Let me reassure you that if, erm should I say, when, John turns up, my good ladies, I will send word immediately to your place of lodging.' His round, ruddy face exuded sincerity.

'For that we thank you, Mr. Dooley.' Mary sighed feeling weary, but hopeful. Kate wrote the name of the hotel for Mr. Dooley and helped her mother to her feet. 'I bid you farewell ladies. May the Lord walk with you.' Dooley waved as they crossed the cobbled courtyard of the mews and returned to Lord St, which was not far from Church St, where they hoped their new hats were waiting.

Chapter 45

Fetching the Daisies

Catherine was enjoying working on the black and scarlet hat. Molly occasionally received such orders, usually from actors passing through the city while performing at the theatre, such flamboyant choice was not common amongst Molly's usual customers. The wide brimmed felt hat was to be one of her most extravagant creations, adorned with copious amounts of lace, feathers and sequins.

'If only we had more orders like this, Cathy,' Molly mused. 'They're such fun to put together, but too brash for our clients. It needs to be ready for the customer later today.'

'I'll have it ready Molly, but don't forget the daisies need fetchin'.'

'Vera can go along with a note. Will you do that Vera?' Molly's request made Vera flinch and her two companions smiled at her reaction. 'Vera luv', your face is almost as scarlet as this feather.' Catherine giggled. 'Mrs. Sanders won't eat you, she's a nice lady.'

Vera had resolved to ensure that Catherine would meet the two ladies she had missed yesterday; she was convinced that they were connected in some way to Catherine and her family. What if they arrived while she was collecting the daisies? They would take their hats and leave without Catherine ever knowing they existed.

'A trip out won't hurt you Vera, it'll be good for your confidence. I'll write it all down for you and it's not much of a walk to Paradise St, so stop worrying! I'm going to open up now. Catherine you get on with the sequins. Vera take the note and the cash round to Mrs. Sanders now, you can't get on without the daisies.'

Vera shook her head panicking, she needed to get her message across, but Molly became impatient: 'Vera! Go now!' she ordered, opening the door and gently pushing the distressed girl out onto the already busy Church St. 'What is wrong with that child?' Molly asked herself, reaching for the order book. 'Such a strange one.'

Catherine had already stitched half the sequins onto her project for the day and was completely absorbed in her work, so much so that she failed to notice the two women enter the shop, and was oblivious to the fact that her aunt and grandmother, whose existence she scarcely knew of, were within yards of where she was seated.

'Ahh yes the daisies Mrs. Sanders concurred, reading Molly's note. I've a box here, ordered far too many. We're having a run on lavender for the bonnets and soon I'll be ordering the autumn stock, fruit and nuts.' She smiled at the silent, unresponsive child. 'Sally, go and fetch the box of daisies I left ready on the table in the back for Molly Briers.'

Sally, a sullen, freckled red head, darted an unfriendly glance at Vera and ambled slowly into the back room of the shop, in no hurry to comply with the wish of her employer.

'So you're Vera?' Mrs. Sanders mused in a kindly manner. Molly told me about you. Said you don't talk. Well that's a blessing as far as I'm concerned. Some people never stop talking and most of the time it's drivel. Molly says you're a good worker, that's what matters.' Sally arrived with the box of daisies and resumed her position behind the counter.

'There you are. One box of daisies, various sizes.' Vera had waited patiently for the transaction to be completed, but now took the box from Mrs. Sanders and hastily handed her the money. 'Oh! Almost forgot, Mrs. Sanders cried, placing the cash in her till. I've a little something extra for Molly. I think she'll like it. One moment Vera. Sally, watch the shop while I nip upstairs.'

Vera had no choice but to remain, her heart breaking as she thought about the terrible missed opportunity that was occurring at Molly's shop, knowing that by now the two women would have returned to collect their hats and Catherine would be working on the scarlet hat in the back room.

After what seemed like an eternity, Mrs. Sanders

returned carrying another box: 'I made this for Molly at the weekend. It's a fruit cake. She asked me for the recipe, last time we took tea together, of course the recipe is my little secret.' Mrs. Sanders smiled conspiratorially, placing her index finger on her lips. Vera nodded and aware that her countenance was again as scarlet as the feathers soon to be adorning Catherine's hat. She took the fruitcake and daisies and sped as fast as she could along Paradise St, dodging the bustle of people and carriages, back to Church St, almost stumbling on the dewy cobbles as she arrived at Molly's shop, bursting in to the surprise of Molly and her two customers.

'Vera!' Molly shrilled. 'You've been racing; no need for such haste my girl. Take the stock to the workroom while I deal with these worthy ladies.' Still flushed, Vera looked intently from one lady to the other, and hastened to the workroom where Catherine remained engrossed in the task of adding copious sequins to the now sparkling hat. To her great surprise, Vera grabbed her hand and began pulling her away from the table.

'Vera! What are you doing'?' she shrieked. Vera continued to pull and Catherine sensed danger, never having seen her workmate so animated, let alone be pulled and pushed around in this manner.

Within seconds, Catherine found herself being forced into the shop ahead of Vera, who was pushing the reluctant girl with all her mite.

'Vera!' Molly cried, 'what are you doing?' She was outraged by the behaviour of her young assistant, while Kate and Mary were shocked to see the pale, fair-haired girl hurtling towards them, vehemently resisting the assault.

'Vera stop it!' she pleaded. 'What are you doing? Have you gone completely mad?' Molly was mortified. 'So sorry ladies,' she lamented. 'This is unusual behaviour. Vera, go to the workroom now!' Molly commanded: 'Go!'

Vera's confusion was intense and she stood silent, looking at Molly's angry face and the confused reaction of the two customers and Catherine's wild grey eyes darting from one to the other. She turned to leave, obeying Molly's orders, but on reaching the door, turned again to the astounded tableaux and to the further amazement of Molly and Catherine screeched: 'Catherine Cattell! Catherine Cattell!'

Mary and Kate gasped, Molly and Catherine simultaneously dropped their jaws at the sound of a voice they never thought they would hear coming from the tearful Vera, who, on hearing her own voice, swooned and fell to the floor. Molly ran to her aid, lifting her gently onto a chair. 'Catherine, fetch water. Please excuse Vera's behaviour. She's never uttered a word.

Mary and Kate watched the fair-haired waif with tears welling in their eyes, as the realisation dawned that the gentle girl was John's daughter.

Chapter 46

Old Swan

John had awakened that morning to the sound of cockerels cheerily greeting another day. From his bed, facing a large, low window, he saw a pale, pink sky and distant, grey hills. He contemplated the day ahead, which demanded that he leave the peace behind and make his way into the city. Living temporarily in a cottage he was renting in Old Swan, a village a few miles from the city, the journey on foot would take him two hours at a leisurely pace, but he enjoyed his life beyond the smoke, away from the crowds. In Old Swan, the air was clean and life seemed much simpler, but Ben Dooley would be waiting to complete the book and he had already spent a day longer than usual away from the print works.

Three late days seemed to be acceptable but he supposed his employer would not be amused were he to stretch to a fourth. Besides which, he needed his wages to pay the rent. Within an hour he was on his way along Prescot Rd, passing Tom the blacksmith hammering away beside a huge carthorse waiting to be shod. Tom waved a friendly hello.

'Off to town John?' Tom called.

'Yes Tom, can I bring anything back for you?'

'Some of that good cheese from Cooper's, and a bag of sugar for the wife if it's not too much trouble.'

'Will do Tom. We'll settle up later.'

'Good man!' said the blacksmith, whose hearty countenance, after a lifetime of breathing clean air, bore a stark contrast to the sallow complexions of his city counterparts.

John continued the journey, stopping occasionally to

rest by the roadside, as now and then a coach bumped past. At the coach station he stopped for refreshment. As he reached Kensington, he became aware of the stench of rubbish left on the streets to rot and thought about the children he discarded and how they were surviving in this place of contrasts; where the rich could live such privileged lives and the poor suffered humiliation and neglect. He was feeling strong now, with work and money saved. It was time to reunite, but so far he had not devised a plan to do so.

Dooley's printing shop was close to the Pier Head in mews behind Lord St.

'John! There you are!' Dooley's greeting was unusually enthusiastic.'

'I have the work for you Mr. Dooley. A bit late, for which I apologise, but I hope you'll be satisfied.'

'Splendid!' Dooley responded, genuinely appreciative as he glanced over the etchings. And then with a rare gravitas he turned to the poor man who stood before him.

'Come over here John. I have something to tell you.'

John sat in shocked silence while the story unfolded of how his mother and sister Kate had come looking for him and that they were staying just a few minutes away from where he sat and, as he listened, he was aware that an ending was approaching. Not the ending he had planned, but something different and he was not sure what. He had lost control of the ending, but perhaps that was a good thing. Perhaps he would never have found a way to end his anguish alone.

'They're very worried about you John,' his employer concluded with a deep sigh.

He shook kind Mr. Dooley's hand and, torn by conflicting emotions, set off to find his seekers, little knowing that the two had become three, with the recent addition of Catherine.

Within an hour the reunion took place in the lobby of the hotel and Catherine, overwhelmed with excitement, received the fatherly hug she had longed for, while her grandmother and aunt looked on, bewildered by the account of events to which they were so far privy. There was much more to learn, but for now the four were united in their joy.

Soon they would be joined by Billy and Alfie and there was much healing to undergo. Could Billy ever forgive? It would not be easy and may never happen, but future years would see them back together in the house on Great Newton St, forging the future which would be long and eventful for the boys.

Not so for Catherine.

PART 3

LIVERPOOL 1920

Chapter 47

The office was small and tightly fitted with dark oak cupboards and shelves. A huge desk filled the space in front of the sash window through which light poured. The desk was strewn with posters, price tags and other paraphernalia related to Alfie's occupation as a signwriter at the prestigious Cooper's Grocery store on Church Street.

The man himself was perched on a high stool, deep in concentration as he worked on a sign to advertise the shop's own brand of tea, *Supplied to King Alphonso XIII and the Spanish Household*. That's a lot to fit on a line, I hope King Alphonso enjoys his Cooper's cuppa, thought Alfie. Cooper's was famous for tea and coffee beans; the exotic aroma of the latter was ever present throughout the shop and beyond, enticing Liverpool's elite to gather in the elegant coffee shop just below Alfie's office.

Alfie Cattell was forty years-old, a father of eight and a war veteran, whose artistic talent had brought him to this quiet haven of an office, where he could work in peace and survey the scene beyond his window. Church Street was a popular thoroughfare for shoppers and visitors to the city who gathered in transit to their new lives across the Ocean. Sailors on leave from long voyages flocked to the bars, and horse-drawn carriages vied with fancy new motor cars along the busy road. Alfie enjoyed the vibrant entertainment of the street scenes, often accompanied by live jazz music from the Cooper's Quartet; a stylish group of musicians who played regularly in the café. It seemed everyone wanted to erase the memories of war. Cheer had returned to the streets and it was good to watch from the window.

A knock at the door disturbed his thoughts, and Sam

the messenger popped his head round.

'Y' wife's 'ere Alfie,' he announced. 'Shall I let 'er in?'

'Try keeping her out!' Alfie smiled, putting his pen down.

Sarah bustled in and stood before him looking tousled and harassed, as usual. Mary, their six year-old middle daughter clung to her hand and stood obediently beside her.

'Alf, look after Mary for an hour, there's a sale on at T.J Hughes', a good one. It's like hell in there an' I'll lose her, y' know what she's like for wandr'n off.'

Alfie smiled affectionately at his daughter, who was excited at the thought of spending time with her daddy in his office. 'Go and shop dear one. See if y' can find me some decent black socks. Mine are full of holes.'

'Alf luv, I'll darn y' socks,' Sarah promised, placing a gentle hand on her husband's shoulder. 'Frankie needs shoes an' Mag's outgrowin' everythin'. Your socks are a long way down the list.'

Alfie drew her close and kissed her cheek. 'That's alright beloved. I just make the money. It's a bit much to expect good socks I suppose.' He smiled good humouredly and Sarah giggled as she set off on her mission, leaving the office calm and silent again. Mary clambered onto a stool beside her daddy. She knew not to disturb him as he worked, but loved to watch as he created the stylish store signs for the shop and window display. Occasionally he would light his pipe and enjoy a few puffs, so that the tobacco aroma mingled with the scent of coffee and wood polish. He was smartly dressed with brown pinstriped trousers held up by braces over a starched white shirt. A waste-coat and jacket, presently hung on a hook by the door, completed the dapper look which he and Sarah considered important for his position at Coopers. His fair hair was not yet grey, and his eyes were a pale shade of blue. He turned to Mary, whose eyes were an identical hue and whose pale complexion, framed by fair tendrils, tugged at his heartstrings.

'Are you busy Daddy?' Mary asked, surveying the contents of his desk, always a source of fascination to the inquisitive little girl.

'Busy beyond words Mary. Too busy to ever be finished.' He smiled broadly and Mary rested her head against his arm.

'I won't talk,' she whispered.

'Ahh Cathy, you can talk as much as you like. I love to listen to you,' Alfie murmured, absently, adding a final flourish to King Alphonso's tea poster.

'Cathy?' Mary quizzed. Daddy! I'm Mary. We haven't got a Cathy. Eva, Maggie and me, Mary smiled. Alfie gasped at his mistake.

'Did I call you Cathy? That's the strangest thing. But...' He hesitated. 'You look so much like her.'

'Like who?' Mary laughed at the puzzlement of it all.

'Like Catherine.' Alfie's thoughts were drifting.

'Where is she dad?' Mary persisted curiously.

It was almost too much for Alfie to remember his sister, but his slip of the tongue and Mary's uncanny resemblance to Catherine, brought long suppressed memories racing through his mind.

LIVERPOOL 1893

Chapter 48

Rose petals fell from a clear blue sky and the sun blazed, pushing its rays through the abundantly leafy red beach and silver birch trees that lined the footpath of Saint John's Church, and the bells tolled as the newly-weds emerged, joyfully from the coolness of the church and into the midday June heat.

Colleen and Bernadette, lovely in their simple blue lace trimmed frocks, carried Ethel's train into which petals floated. They were proud of their new step-mother and overjoyed for Paddy, their father, who grinned widely and pulled his bride close as a little gathering of well-wishers flung petals and an Irish fiddler played *The Peacock's Feathers*, an jig that got the feet tapping and promised a good time to be had once a few shots of the hard stuff had been downed at *The Crown*, the designated gathering place which brought the two together.

'It was love at first sight,' Ethel would often recount. 'Love at first sight. I knew we were destined for each other as soon as he walked in the door looking for John Cattell. It's the one good thing about your dad goin' missin' Cathy; if he hadn't, we may never 'ave met.'

Catherine had been reminded of this fact many times; every time she and Ethel met. Luckily she was fond of both Ethel and Paddy, so was able to forgive the fact that the years of heartbreak caused by her father's disappearance had now taken on the happy purpose of matchmaking.

Catherine and her cousin Maude strewed petals on the path and flung them into the air. Gertie, the workhouse nurse, surprised the crowd with a great attempt at an Irish jig, and Alfie, Billy and John Cattell clapped to the tune as the happy couple passed.

Molly Brier's bonnets were flaunted and best taffeta frocks worn, adorned with daisies, buttercups and fragrant wild roses.

The wedding party made their way across the road to *The Crown Inn*, where drinks and pies awaited.

'This is the best day I can remember, ever!' Catherine confided to Maude as they crossed the road, while from tram-tops commuters cheered and waved as the happy couple passed by.

An observer would quickly conclude that the wedding was not a high-class affair, and that the special clothes were simple and brightly coloured, but the joy was evident and worth a thousand of the jewels and riches which may have adorned a high-class equivalent.

'I think you're right Cathy. I'm so happy for Paddy and Ethel, the kindest people in the world. Colleen and Bernie look beautiful,' Maude gushed.

The cousins, Catherine and Maude, linked arms as they entered *The Crown*, Maude's long black hair, thick and lustrous, was tied with a red bow just below her rose adorned bonnet; her dress was simple white cotton. Catherine, although Maud's age at sixteen years appeared to be much younger, slightly built, there was a fragility about her, and today her pale blue frock adorned with forget-me-nots, perfectly complemented her blue eyes and the daisy bonnet, made for her by Molly, created a fresh, summery look that bright June day.

'Sure Cathy! You look like a garden on two legs, so you do,' Colleen had remarked on greeting her at *The Crown*. 'I'll be after watering you so you don't wilt.'

There was singing and dancing; Irish jigs and mournful melodies from his homeland rendered by Paddy, who all agreed had a splendid voice.

Maude was forced to leave early and catch the tram back to Newsham where Mrs. Bagshaw was expecting her return to work in time to serve dinner. Catherine stayed close to her father John, and brothers Billy and Alfie, relishing their time together and the happy circumstances. Could she ever have dreamt of such a thing happening during her days of misery in the workhouse? She looked at Paddy and recalled her first sighting of him in the workhouse chapel, standing beside Billy, as she and Colleen waited to hear Alfie sing in the choir, and Bernie was in the infirmary with pneumonia. Could this be a dream? she thought, smiling as she surveyed the scene before her now; so much joy! For now, she thought, casting a sisterly glance towards her little brothers Billy and Alfie, whom she had mothered since their own mother fell ill and passed away... for now, all is well. And that was as much as she could hope, for she was aware of the fickleness of life and took no happy moment for granted.

'Would you like to dance?' The question emerged through the fiddle music and the din of happy chatter, and Catherine was surprised to find it was directed at her. It came from a young man she had noticed earlier among Ethel's family group; dark featured with smiling eyes and a kind face. They had exchanged a glance or two, but Catherine thought little of it until now.

'Yes thank you, I would,' she replied, feeling a rush of blood to her cheeks. A boy had asked her to dance!

'I'm Tom,' he told her as they swung to an Irish jig.'Tom Duke, Ethel's nephew.'

'Pleased to meet you Tom,' Catherine shyly responded as the music stopped and she slipped quietly back to her seat beside her father, aware of the fluttering of her heartbeat and the wide eyes and raised eyebrows of Bernie and Colleen, both of whom had noticed the spark of attraction between their friend an Tom.

Outside, the sun that had blazed so gloriously on Paddy and Ethel's happy day, drifted serenely to the horizon, leaving a peachy glow of a job well done, above the grandeur of Saint George's Hall and the guests, hearts full of love, dispersed and returned to the reality of their daily grind.

Chapter 49

Tom

Tom Duke was the son of Ethel's younger sister, Harriet and her husband Andrew. He had eight siblings, all living at home in three rooms on Scotland Road, not far from Paddy and his family. He worked as a delivery boy for Cooper's Grocery Store on Church Street, and had often seen Catherine coming and going from Molly Briar's Hat Shop.

He first noticed her the day of the terrible storm that had drifted out to sea and taken the lives of many poor sailors. She and Molly had been sweeping water away from the shop, and the two of them were laughing as they tried to battle the torrent. That was some time ago, and ever since he had watched for her every day, unbeknown to Catherine.

He was surprised to see her at his Auntie Ethel's wedding, not knowing there was any potential way of connecting with the pretty, delicate sweet girl of his dreams, but fate had very kindly brought him to her.

'Saw you dancin' with that Cathy Cattell,' his brother George commented, as they made their way home from the wedding.

'What of it?' Tom retorted, annoyed at his brother's unkind tone.

'Nowt really. She's ex-workhouse, same as Paddy,' George remarked with the faint hint of a sneer. Tom had not known this about Catherine, and his heart pounded with the shock of it. 'That's sad,' he said. 'I hope she didn't suffer much.'

Chapter 50

Molly's Shop

Molly's hats had grown so popular, that she and her workers Vera and Catherine, hardly had time to breath once the day got underway. A new dynamic had entered the scene that spring in the shape of Mr. Entwistle, Molly's new suiter. He came from Manchester and travelled to Liverpool by train every weekend to stay at the affluent Adelphi Hotel, and escort Molly to fashionable events, concerts, art exhibitions, lectures. Molly was besotted, and talked endlessly about him and the world he had opened up to her; the art of Augustus John, the dream world of Jung, the writings of Charles Dickens.

'Fascinating!' she would gasp, as Vera and Catherine stitched. 'Charles Dickens writes about poor people like you two. People in the workhouse! Would you believe it?' Vera and Catherine exchanged glances. They felt uncomfortable about Molly's constant reminders of the past they would both like to forget, and they suspected something unsettling about her darling Mr. Henry Entwistle.

'See the way he lords it around the shop!' Vera whispered one afternoon when he was visiting the premises. 'I think he's got his mind set on more than Molly, Cathy. I'm sure as 'owt he's set on the taking over the business.' Catherine and Vera studied Mr. Entwistle as he examined every nook and cranny of Molly's shop with great interest.

'What's 'e thinking' Vera?' the friends exchanged worried glances.

Their fears were justified as, at the end of August and after the summer bonnet rush, Molly announced her engagement to Mr. Entwistle, and broke the dreadful news that she would be moving the business to Manchester.

'It makes sense girls,' she told them. 'Once I'm married and the children come along, I'll need Henry to run the business at times. You can come with me of course, I'll not find workers like the two of you easily, and there'll be rooms for you to lodge on the premises.'

Reluctantly Vera, having no family or other option but to return to the workhouse, accepted the offer, but Catherine refused to leave her newly re-formed family. By October of that year, Molly Brier's Hat Shop had gone from Church Street, and Catherine was out of a job.

With Alfie and her father both working for Mr. Dooley, the printer, and Billy enrolled with a new ship, *The Indian Princess*, money was adequate and she was able to stay home and take care of the house. She took some seamstress work from a local dressmaker, which would occupy her late into the evening. She missed Vera, Molly and the hats, but adjusted to the new routine of cleaning, cooking and stitching. With autumn upon them, life in the household fell into a pattern, hardly imaginable one year earlier. Had anyone told Catherine, during the workhouse years, that a day would come when she would watch Alfie and her father set off together for work, while Billy was happily employed by another generous captain, she would have considered it the stuff of dreams, but here she was, living that dream. Although some more privileged folk may have considered her existence to be more akin to a nightmare; cleaning, washing and cooking by day, then stitching by night. Her sewing work was provided by Mrs. Brown, a tiny lady, not much taller that her kitchen table, with a countenance as straight as the seams she demanded. Catherine was reminded of Miss Clancy, her sewing mistress at the workhouse, who had prepared her well for the high standards of Mrs. Brown. 'I'll pay you threepence for every straight seam and expect twenty seams weekly from you,' she instructed shrilly. Twenty seams required the burning of a few candles, as Catherine could only settle to her stitching in the evenings after the supper plates were cleaned.

'Catherine, lass! There's no need for you to sew seams. We're not short of money,' her father remonstrated.

'Don't worry daddy. I could never be a lady of leisure

and we can use the money toward good shoes for Alf and Bill.'

Chapter 51

John

There were times John was able to see the sense of his present state of being, and weeks when he would move through time like a man in control and content with his destiny, but there were also dark times of resentment and haunting memories.

Two wives lost to the same cruel disease, and rebuilding his life twice over. Once, America had beckoned and he held in his hand a ticket to sail, but tossed it to a young beggar, whose dejected soul sparkled at the chance to escape the city that had left him behind as it forged its glorious future. John had never received such sincere thanks, or witnessed such joy that he saw on the face of the youth as he ran towards *The Liverpool Lady*, leaving the true owner of the ticket to turn away and seek his family: the call of duty; a burden or a gift?

There was also, among his memories, the joy he witnessed on Catherine's face when they were re-united, possibly as complete as the young beggar's. Was that the exchange? He considered this for a while. His sacrifice had resulted in bringing happiness to others, twice over, therefore his decision had been right. Better to bring joy than leave sadness. Alfie was starting to trust him now and was learning the trade well. He was a talented artist and the copperplate handwriting taught in the workhouse would be a source of income for him in years to come. Billy, had yet to forgive him, and may never do so. This he had accepted. It seemed there was nothing he could say to remove the anger from his eyes. He missed Old Swan and the cottage he had rented before moving back to town; waking up to the cock crow and the slower pace of country life. Sometimes he would walk there with Alfie and Catherine, to escape the smoggy city. Fresh air was good for body and soul.

But there was something troubling John; an uneasiness, something he was not willing to acknowledge and now he was denying his suspicions. If he did that, then surely they would disappear.

LIVERPOOL 1920

Chapter 52

A Revelation

'Look at me! I'm caked in muck from that infernal road. Too many carriages, trams and cars to dodge, and ankle high in horse manure, it's surprising any poor soul without wheels survives.' Sarah was laden with bags and boxes, tied up with string. 'I've had a good morning though. Town's full of bargains today. C'mon Mary, there's a tram to Old Swan at two o'clock. I've to get back and start the tea.' Mary reluctantly jumped down from her stool. The quiet times spent watching her father at work were rare and she cherished them.

'Daddy,' she whispered, as Alfie put down his paint brush. 'Who's Catherine?' She saw her father's face sadden; a rare moment when he was taken off guard.

'She was my big sister, Mary,' he answered, softly.

'And where is she now?' Mary ventured. Sensing her father's despair.

'She died, Mary.' There were tears in his eyes and silence in the room.

'How did she die?' Mary asked, her voice trembling as she drew the memory from her dear father who it seemed was no longer fully present. She saw the tear on his cheek and her mother, unmoving, laden with packages, watching her husband; together with him in that moment of painful remembrance.

'Well Mary,' he finally spoke, gazing into his daughter's soft blue eyes. 'She died of a broken heart.'

LIVERPOOL 1891

Chapter 53

A Stormy Night

'Perfect Miss Catherine, a perfect seam,' sighed Mrs. Brown, ecstatically. 'A rarity, I can tell you!' She and Catherine were seated in her small abode amongst piles of fabric and a variety of dress-making paraphernalia, which encroached the living space so much that the two were perched on stacks of muslin and crepe of many hues. Mrs. Brown lived her work, often the case for dressmakers, with many important deadlines to meet. A wedding or funeral dress delivered a day late would be the ruin of her business. She ate, slept and worked in the same room, which reflected her modest income, as well as her taste for the fashionable clutter found in most houses in the Victorian era; walls filled with heavily framed pictures of angels, sweet children, crinoline clad women sporting huge floral hats, and of course Queen Victoria sternly watching over the activity within the humble little space, as if every dress was for her royal self. There were numerous naked statues of the Greek and Roman variety, over which were draped yards of fabric and a treadle operated sewing machine, which had pride of place in the bay window.

'Where did y'learn such stitchin'?' Mrs. Brown asked the windswept Catherine. November had roared in with stormy weather that kept the populace at home, and only the brave or desperate were setting foot beyond their own walls. Catherine was neither of these, but she had a sense of duty and had promised Mrs. Brown the finished work on that day, so had no choice but to battle the gale for the hundred yards or so to reach her house.

'Had a strict teacher; Miss Clancy, in the workhouse.'

Catherine answered unashamedly. She was always ready to praise her teacher, in spite of the fear the strict woman had instilled in many of the girls. Miss Clancy had given her a skill and a means of surviving beyond the workhouse. She owed a great deal to the woman.

'Oh yes, I've 'ad a few trained by her. At least y' learned a trade in y' hard times,' Mrs. Brown pronounced; her face very close to Catherine's as she emphasised her final words.

There was no time for niceties, and Mrs. Brown paid Catherine the shilling owed for her work and escorted her to the door. Catherine re-joined the windy drama out on the street. Clinging to the iron railings, she pulled herself up to the top of the hill as the force of the gale almost lifted her off her feet and took her breath away. With just a few more feet to go the strength began to ebb from her until she lost her grip and, terrified, began to succumb, falling prey to the invisible grasp of a particularly strong gust, her seemingly feather-light body was caught by strong hands, which steadied her.

'I've got you Catherine, you're safe!' A voice re-assured her, and she turned to see Tom, sheltering her in a calm oasis as the storm raged.

'Tom! Thank goodness you're here! I thought I was finished'' she cried, exhausted.

'Let's get you home, girl. Why you're out on a night as bad as this, I don't know.' They leaned into the wind together and finally reached the safety of Catherine's house.

John was working by lamp light at the kitchen table with young Alfie looking on, and was shocked to see the dishevelled pair enter. Tom led Catherine to a chair and gently removed her cape and hat, while she struggled for breath.

'Where've you been Cathy? I'd no idea you'd left the house! What were you thinking of on a night like this?' John was shocked at the sight of his daughter. 'You're white as a sheet luv, catch your breath and I'll make a brew.'

'I'd to take the dresses to Mrs. Brown, Dad. She needed them for picking up tomorrow,' Catherine panted. 'The wind would have taken me, for sure, if Tom hadn't been there at the right time.' John's gratitude was abundant as he shook the young man's hand. He remembered him from Paddy's wedding, and how he seemed to have taken a fancy to

Catherine.

'Can't thank you enough lad,' he gushed. 'I'd no idea she was out in that storm.' Soon there was ale on the table and conversation flowing, and when the storm subsided, Tom made his way home, trying to recall why he had been out in the storm and heading up Great Newton Street, when he came across Catherine, but he could think of no reason other than it was meant to be.

LIVERPOOL 1912

Chapter 54

'She said Old Swan will be good for him Alf. Cleaner air. More chance of his lungs healing,' Sarah whispered as Alfie stoked the stove in search of more heat in their living room.

The children were sleeping, although William's coughing served as a constant reminder of the reason why the family would have to leave their home in the city where Sarah and Alfie had grown up a few streets from each other, and moved from their childhood homes into the cosy terraced house on Smithdown Lane to begin their married life, and their family. First James, then William, Alfie junior and baby Evalyn. They had thought that the little house would be their home long into the future, but recently the doctor had confirmed their greatest fear, one that Alfie had hoped to never encounter again; the killer that had slunk through his family, tearing it apart and destroying the bond between father and sons in its wake. He smoked his pipe and contemplated the flames. Sarah sensed where his thoughts had wandered and left him in peace, while firelight flickered on the brass ornaments, polished daily, to keep the bright shine which she never allowed to dull; as if the shine symbolised their love and should never be neglected. She busied herself with the endless task of sock darning. Finally Alfie raised his blue eyes and met the deep brown stare of his beloved Sarah.

'If Miss Bevan says so, and is kind enough to find us a house in Old Swan, then we have no choice but to go my love. Old Swan's a long way out, but trams will get me into town for work and if it rids our William of this cursed illness, it'll be worth the trouble.' Sarah smiled, relieved. It would be a wrench to leave the old familiar places, but she felt there was hope to be found in Ulster Road, where Margaret Bevan, the kind lady who was doing so much to help the likes of William, had arranged for them to re-locate, and once Sarah's mind was made up, Alfie knew there would be no changing it.

The second daughter of her Irish mother and Scottish father, James Duncan, Sarah had always been headstrong; a fact that came to light when, at the age of twelve after the death of her mother, she was beckoned to Dundalk in Ireland to live on the family farm with her grandparents. Months later, to everyone's astonishment and the consternation of her grandparents, she appeared at her father's doorstep on Peach Street, having fled the farm and returned to Liverpool alone.

'If you try to send me back dad, I'll run away again, so you'll just have to put up with me,' she announced, and James knew there was no point in arguing. Sarah found work as a trainee confectioner and soon after that, met Alfie Cattell, the love of her life.

LIVERPOOL 1893

Chapter 55

Sweet Sarah

So far, it had been a good day for thirteen year-old Alfie. The new Liverpool football team was in the Second Division of the Football League and doing well. He was still faithful to Everton and undecided about which team would eventually win his full loyalty. Pondering this on a drizzly October afternoon, post-match with lovebirds Billy and Colleen in tow, he felt a sudden surge of elation while the misty rain gently bathed his face.Hands thrust in his pockets, it was one of those rare days when all was well with the world, and he was acutely aware of the fact. Such awareness may be reserved only for those who have experienced the opposite, and Alfie had suffered his share of adversity during his troubled early years. Who would have thought, during the bleakness of his days in the workhouse, that one day he would stroll along London Road with his brother and Colleen, carefree and at one with the world?

'You're look'n very pleased with y'self, so y'are Alfie Cattell.' Colleen chirped. He blushed, never liking attention, but sent her a smile and a nod, never-the-less.

'Let him enjoy the moment Colleen. He's stuck on that new team an' they just won a match, but they'll never replace Everton,' Billy teased.

They turned the corner into Great Newton Street and Colleen slipped into Sadie Smith's, the baker's shop.

'I promised me Da' I'd bring him back a Battenberg for tea,' she informed them. The boys followed her in, eyeing the colourful display of cakes with disinterest. Shopping was Catherine's territory, and cakes were not commonly found in their household.

'What can I do f' yer?' Sadie Smith asked, proudly arranging a batch of buns upon a plate perched on the counter top. She wore a white cotton apron over her ankle length black dress, and a white bonnet from which no hair protruded, giving the impression that only her good humoured smile had escaped the strictures of her dress code.

'Well now,' she beamed broadly. 'If it isn't that Billy and Alfie Cattell! How's y'dad and that lovely sister of yours?' Sadie knew the family and was aware of their troubled history. She surveyed the boys with sympathetic eyes. 'You've grown to be fine young lads an' yer mam, God rest 'er sweet soul, would be proud of yez. She was a good friend of mine, taken too soon.' Billy and Alfie smiled in acknowledgement of the kind words. They were accustomed to this treatment in the local shops, whose workers remembered their family before tragedy divided them. Colleen waited patiently for the Battenberg.

'Sarah!' Sadie bellowed, with a voice intended to reach the back room where her young assistant Sarah Duncan was busy icing a wedding cake. 'Bring me that apple pie y'made earlier. You boys can take it home. Tell y'dad it's a gift from me.' Sarah emerged from the back room, the apple pie balanced on her right hand, an icing knife firmly gripped in the other, brown eyes, a mop of black hair pulled back into a tight bun and a broad smile. The sudden arrival of this bundle of energy, startled Alfie.

'There y'go Sadie. One apple pie. Where d'y'want it?' Sarah enquired, flourishing the pie in the air as if it were a platter of precious jewels.

'Put it in a bag an' give it to Alfie here,' Sadie instructed, indicating the slender, blue eyed boy who stood already besotted by the young girl who, on this day of universal blessings, had instantly intensified the warm glow of joy already in situ within his heart. He watched her slide the pie into a paper bag, completely unaware that she had changed his life.

'There y'are Alfie. All yours.' She handed him the pie and was gone in an instant. 'I'll 'ave this cake finished within the hour Sadie,' she called as she left the shop and returned to her work in the back room.

'That's very kind of you Mrs. Smith,' Alfie stammered, blushing uncontrollably. 'Let me pay you for it.'

'It's a gift Alf luv. Y'mam was my friend. Take it home an' enjoy it on me.' Sadie smiled kindly.

'Sure, Mrs. Smith, I'll take the Battenberg now. If it's not too much trouble,' Colleen cut in, still patiently awaiting her dad's treat.

'Sorry Colleen luv. One Battenberg comin' up!' Sadie laughed.

As they left Sadie's shop, laden with apple pie and cake, Alfie carried another delicious dish homeward; a syrupy sweet dollop of everlasting love.

The house on Great Newton Street had almost resumed the lost ambience John and his children had yearned for since the death of Anne Marie. Their kitchen was often inhabited by friends; Tom, Maude, Colleen, Bernie, Paddy, Ethel, Russian Alex and more recently, piles of penny buns, with the occasional Victoria sponge cake appearing, courtesy of Alfie, a puzzling development, until he arrived home one evening with Sarah, the young confectioner. It had required many trips to Sadie's shop and a great deal of shyness to overcome, but Alfie had finally managed to woo her and her appearance at the Great Newton Street table was an undisputed success.

Chapter 56

Ireland Beckons

September winds gave way to prolonged rains and the high street stores enjoyed bumper sales of umbrellas and boots as pitted lanes and alleyways became puddle strewn and rivulets of water ran along the cobbles, while ragged shoeless children splashed their cold, bare feet in deep pools of freezing water. It was around that time that Paddy and Ethel announced the news that they were expecting a baby in the spring, and Colleen and Bernadette were summoned to Ireland to help their grandmother on her farm in Wicklow.

'Why would you want to go there?' Catherine asked incredulously, feeling a surge of sadness and fear that they may never return. She had remained good friends with the sisters and could hardly imagine life in Liverpool without them around, besides which, she knew Billy was head over heels in love with Colleen.

'Our Granda's sick, so he is, and Grandma needs help on the farm. She wrote to me da' to ask if we'd go over, and we sometimes get the feel'n we're in the way a bit now Ethel's moved in an' with the new babby comin' and all.' Bernie attempted to be cheerful, but did not fool Catherine, who sensed her reluctance. They were in Catherine's kitchen drinking sarsaparilla while Catherine sewed the seams of a white frock for Mrs Brown. Her sewing had stopped abruptly on hearing their news.

'Have you told Billy yet Colleen?' she asked, knowing how loaded a question it was.

'No, and please don't mention it Cathy. Not yet; I'll choose my time.' Colleen answered dryly.

'So when will you go?' Catherine asked reluctantly, knowing how painful the answer could be and sure she would fall apart within seconds of hearing it.

'Next week Cathy. Grandma said she needs help urgently and me Da's bought the tickets.' Colleen avoided making eye contact with her dear friend, aware of the deep impact her words would have.

'So soon' was all Catherine managed to say. The sisters took her hands and held them tightly, and the three young friends had no need to communicate their thoughts as each recalled their last parting at the workhouse gate, when Catherine was left behind.

'Sure, it'll not be for long Cathy,' Bernie whispered, afraid the tears would break through her bravado.

'You could come and visit,' Colleen added cheerily, but her heart was breaking at the prospect of leaving Catherine and her darling Billy.

'It won't be forever,' Catherine smiled. 'It wasn't the last time we parted and it won't be this time. You'll be back before I've missed you,' she added reassuringly.

'Ay, to be sure!' the sisters chimed. 'We'll call in before we go Cathy!' And they left as the rain fell like arrows from above, pounding the street with relentless force.

'Goodbye my dear, dear friends,' Catherine sighed as Bernie gently closed the door.

That evening Billy returned home crestfallen and retreated to his room without a word. His beautiful Colleen was leaving. There was nothing more to say.

Chapter 57

November 1892

'Take one of those Victoria sandwich cakes with you Sarah luv,' Sadie suggested as she packed the remaining stock away in the pantry. It was Saturday evening and she was ready to close the shop. 'Give it to Alfie and tell 'im to give Billy a big slice. Poor fella.' Sarah had been telling Sadie about Colleen's departure and Billy's depression.

'It's been six week now an' Alfie says 'e doesn't speak or eat, Sade. Just mopes around.' She was cleaning the counter, absently.

'God luv 'im.' Sadie declared.

Sarah took the Victoria sponge to Alfie's house after work, as instructed, and was surprised to find Catherine, Alfie and Billy happily chatting together around the table.

'Well now, it's nice to see you smiling, Billy. I thought that smile had gone forever. Has Everton had a win? Sadie sent this to cheer you up.' Sarah announced setting the Victoria sponge cake down on the table and searching for a knife to cut it.

'That's exactly what we need to celebrate Billy's good news,' said Catherine laughing and reaching for a stack of the best China plates and a doilies. 'That cake needs some special treatment, and so does Billy.'

Billy had a pile of documents in front of him on the table, and was busy thumbing through them. Alfie was also studying them with interest.

'He's been signed up with the Lucky Shamrock, A steamer that goes back and forth to Dublin an' you can guess why that makes him happy.' Alfie explained.

'That's the best news I've heard in a long time. Colleen will explode with joy, so she will!' Sarah bubbled, good humouredly mimicking Colleen's Irish brogue, which set them all laughing.

'Thanks Sarah! I have to say it's a long time since I felt this way. Life doesn't seem right without my Colleen. I can get shore leave over in Dublin and easily travel to Wicklow by train to visit her.'

'When will you start?' Sarah asked, tucking into a large slice off Jammy sponge cake.

'Next week if all goes well,' Billy answered. "We set sail Mondays and back Fridays. I'll call in on Paddy and Ethel to let them know I'm going. Paddy might want me to take a letter.'

'Great idea Bill. We can send something over for Christmas. I'll make some handkerchiefs.' Billy's news acted as a tonic for the whole family, and Bernie and Colleen's absence didn't seem so drastic after all.

Chapter 58

A New Life in Old Swan

The green fields and leafy lanes of Old Swan were a stark contrast to their old city life, and Sarah's children enjoyed playing out on the street. Billy stayed for a while in the Broadgreen sanatorium, where his health began to improve. Alfie joined the Bowling Club at the Blackhorse pub opposite the blacksmith's, where young Alf junior would stand and gawp for hours watching the smithy at his craft. Sarah quickly made friends with her neighbours. She missed her old life, but William looked so much better, she could hardly complain.She baked a special cake for Christmas and the neighbours, enticed by the aroma of spices, fruit and rum, couldn't help but notice they had a skilled confectioner amongst them.

Mary was born in September, 1914, two months after her father, Alfie had left to join the fight. She would be four years-old before she saw him walking across High Field at the top of Ulster Road. Home from the War.

Sarah's war was over. Little William had survived the white plague and her Alfie had survived the horrors of the front line in France. There was still healing to be done. It would be a while before Alfie was himself again, but his job at Cooper's Store was waiting for him, and he would soon return to the old routine, in spite of the mental war scars he would carry with him for the rest of his life.

Chapter 59

Letters from Wicklow 1893

3rd December 1893

Dearest Catherine,

I couldn't believe my eyes when Billy turned up at the farm my heart skipped a few beats I can tell you.

Bernie and I have been run ragged since we came. Milking cows, feeding chickens, cooking and cleaning. We thought we had it bad in the old workhouse, but after a day here I was wishing we were back there.

Granddad and grandma are both sick so we are trying to keep everything going but it's so hard. The hills are lovely around Wicklow I wish you could see how beautiful it is here I suppose it makes up for all the drudgery. I miss you so much.

Thank you for the handkerchiefs.

Blessings to you and yours for Christmas and the new year.

Your loving friend forever

Colleen

P.S. Bernie has a beau! I'm telling you in secret, because she told me not to mention it to anyone but I can't hold it in.

3rd December 1893

Dearest Catherine,

it was great to see Coleen light up when Billy arrived. She's been so down in the dumps since arriving here. Our days are full of chores from dawn until we fall into bed at sundown. Granddad and Grandma are very sick and can't cope with the farm anymore. I don't know what we can do it's too much for us.

How are you Catherine? It's been so long since we saw you. On Sundays we finish half day and go out to the Hills or to the seaside at Bray which is great.

I'm going to tell you my secret because I am guessing Coleen will tell you anyway, even though she has been sworn to secrecy. I've met a fella and I'm in love. His name is Seamus he is so handsome Cathy and altogether perfect.

I hope you'll come and visit. We miss you and the Mersey and the family.

Thank you for the handkerchief. Miss Clancy would be proud.

Bless you Catherine

your loving friend

Bernie

Catherine couldn't stop herself from smiling as she read the letters Billy had brought back with him.

'Oh Billy, it's so nice to hear from our girls. They seem to be working hard.' Catherine was trying to warm herself by the fireside. She couldn't stop shivering and was wrapped in the thick woollen shawl Billy brought back from Dublin for her. She had been working extra hard to keep up with the Christmas orders from Mrs Brown. Her fingers ached and she felt weary to the bone. She had a cough that had been lingering for a while now, which prevented her from sleeping well and knew it was time to see a doctor.

'Tell me about Ireland Billy, the girls make it sound lovely.' Catherine asked, pulling the shawl tightly round her shoulders. Billy noticed how pale she was and a sudden, dreadful thought crossed his mind. Could it be that their Catherine had something seriously wrong? Half the populous of Liverpool suffered from bronchial problems, so a cough was not unusual, but she looked so thin now. He dismissed the unwanted notion.

'You would love it Cathy. Colleen has a horse an' she gallops around the farm like she was born to it, but the work is wearing them down. I'll be going back there in two weeks and I'll take a letter if you'd like. I could only stay a couple of hours, but I gave them a hand with a few things around the place.'

John and Alfie arrived home from Dooley's print works. They had been working overtime to keep up with the Christmas demand for festive greeting cards and posters. The November rain had given way to freezing weather.

'Dear God, it's cold out there. Pile some coal on the stove Cathy, my feet are aching with frost bite. Dooley's place is like the arctic.' John had interrupted Billy, who was not willing to stay around to hear his father complain.

'I am away out now Catherine. I'll call on Paddy and Ethel to tell them about life on the farm. Then I'll be meeting a few pals for a pint of beer at *The Crown*.' He cast a disdainful glance in his father's direction, and fixing his cap and scarf to keep from freezing, he stepped out, passing Tom on the doorstep. 'Tom lad! Good to see you!,' he greeted warmly, slapping Tom on the back. 'Cathy's ailing a bit. The girl works too hard.'

'Billy boy! How was Ireland? Did you get to see the girls?' Tom responded with equal warmth shaking Billy's hand enthusiastically.

'I did Tom,' Billy answered brightly. 'Catherine will tell you all about it. I've got a few things to do so I'll be off. See you next time mate!'

By the time Tom reached the kitchen, Catherine was putting out the bowls ready to serve the scouse that had been simmering on the stove. Alfie and John were ready to start their meal.

'Hello there Tom boy, sit yourself down and have a bowl of stew.' John invited, genuinely pleased to see him. Catherine took his coat and cap, giving him a gentle kiss on his freezing cheek.

'Thank you John. It's mighty cold out there.' Tom declared, rubbing his hands to get the circulation moving. 'What's this I hear about you being sick Catherine? Billy tells me you're a bit under the weather?' Catherine was surprised by his remark, as Billy had not mentioned anything about her health.

'Oh, it's just a mild flu Tom. I'll be fine by the morning, come and sit down at the table and join us for dinner. How was your day?' She answered avoiding the subject of her health.

John shifted uncomfortably in his chair. Unwilling to look at Catherine for fear of what he might detect. He had been concerned about her health for some time, and tried hard to ignore his imaginings. She was too pale and becoming more delicate than ever. John knew the signs of consumption, how could he not recognise them in his darling Catherine?

'It's been a mad, busy day in the town and I haven't stopped working since 8 o'clock this morning. Everyone needs a turkey delivered, and all the trimmings, so me and the bike have been on the road all day. This scouse is exactly what I need Cathy my love,' Tom answered cheerfully. His cheeks were ruddy with being out in the cold all day, and in contrast to Catherine, he was the picture of health.

After the meal Alfie announced that he had to go to Sarah's house because her father needed help with some painting and decorating he had started and wanted to finish it before Christmas. 'I won't be home late daddy, we have an early start again in the morning remember,' Alfie called on his way out.

'We have indeed young man," John responded. 'Say hello to that girl of yours from me.'

When Alfie had gone, John found a couple of bottles of beer and invited Tom to drink with him. Tom enjoyed a bottle with him and announced his departure.

'Well Catherine it's time I went home. I have another early start tomorrow also, those turkeys won't deliver themselves. you keep warm now and get better soon. I'll call in after work to see how you are. Good night John thank you for the hospitality.'

'You're always welcome here Tom. Take care on that bike of yours,' John replied, and allowing the two young lovers some time alone on the door step, he busied himself clearing the table and washing the dishes. Catherine must rest, he thought.

Tom held Catherine close to him for a while in silence, feeling the warmth off her fragile form. 'You mustn't linger here sweetheart, I'm worried about you. Make sure you keep warm and don't go out tomorrow. My boss has promised me two turkeys if I stay on top of all the deliveries. That will be one for my mam and one for you. Goodnight my lovely,' he kissed her lips gently.

'Goodnight Tom, I'll see you tomorrow,' Catherine sighed, contentedly. She felt such love for her Tom as she watched him bump along the cobbles on his bike, that all thoughts of being poorly went from her mind.

It was the last time she would see him alive.

Chapter 60

A Tragedy

With four days to go before the great Christmas shut down, the frenzy in the city was reaching a climax. There was a fair on in town, and people had flocked from all over Liverpool and beyond, to join the fun. Christmas trees and holly for sale on every corner blocked the pavements, forcing people to walk on the road where horse-drawn carriages vied for space with the busy trams. There was music everywhere; accordion players and pipers vied for audio space and filled the air with every Christmas song imaginable. Hot chestnuts and mulled wine sent sweet and spicy aromas drifting through the ice cold streets; Bold Street was a picture postcard with bunting and fake snow frosting shop windows and Saint Luke's Church at the top of the hill watched over the shoppers and reminded them of the real reason for Christmas, by ringing its bells every hour.

Tom had twenty turkeys to deliver that day and was doing well, with only five to go. He had cycled to the top of Mount Pleasant and delivered two birds and a ham. Three more journeys should do it today, he thought, then he could go to Catherine's and see how she was doing. The more he thought about her, the more he knew he was in love, but he also knew she was sick. Why was she so pale of late? He didn't recall her being quite so thin when she worked at Molly's shop. Could it be that there was something more serious the matter? The thoughts distracted him as he cycled down Bold Street on his way back to Cooper's, and had picked up too much speed to be able to stop when he saw the carriage crossing the bottom of the hill. Within seconds, to the horror of all those in the vicinity, he crashed and was dead before anyone could reach his broken body.

Chapter 61

A Cruel Loss

Tom's death was a cruel loss for all who knew him. A young, healthy life taken too soon; a Christmas tragedy in the midst of joyful anticipation for the big day, Liverpool paused. Tom was a popular boy and well-known around the city as the delivery lad who always smiled to greet you. A bright light extinguished, taking with it some of the sparkle from many lives, and for some there were no words to describe their terrible loss.

The Duke clan on Scotland Road and beyond were bereft. They gathered at his home for the wake; all thoughts of Christmas gone from their minds. The funeral took place at Saint Peter's Church, a stone's throw from Cooper's, where Tom had worked. Many kind people contributed, so that his send off, the day after Boxing day, was a *Grand Affair for a Poor Boy*, according to the *Liverpool Echo*.

Catherine was inconsolable. Nothing anyone could do or say would stem her grief. Her Tom was gone and life had lost its lustre. Maude stayed at the house, sharing her bed to be with her through the awful nights when Catherine's body would shiver with shock. But it was her silence that caused the most concern. Since John had broken the news, she had not uttered a word.

'Oh Billy, it's like she was in the workhouse. Remember that Bernie? She never spoke a word for weeks until she saw Alfie in the choir.' Colleen recalled. Billy was on shore leave in Dublin the weekend after Tom's death and had just delivered the tragic news to the sisters.

'Poor Tom, such a lovely fella. His folks must be beside

themselves; there's never a good way to go, but so sudden, like that, and at Christmas time. It's a cruel blow, sure enough, and Catherine so happy since they met. What will she do Bill?'

Bernie's question was rhetorical. She knew there was no simple answer and Billy was as lost for ideas as anyone.

'There's another thing,' he ventured, hesitantly. 'She's sick.' Billy's head was bowed.

'Sick Billy? What d'ya mean by sick? How sick?' Colleen was panicking now.

'It's hard to say. A lot of the time she has a fever, like the flu and she shivers. But lately she's been coughing at night and is always exhausted.' Billy knew what he was describing. He knew in his heart what was wrong with Catherine, but the thought of it was unbearable.

'Dear God Billy! Do you think it's the consumption she's got?' Bernie asked pointedly. 'If it is, she needs a doctor and must be cared for.' The three fell into silent contemplation.

'Billy, I'm comin' home with you,' Colleen finally announced. 'Bernie, you and Seamus will look after the farm. You can work it out between you. I'm packin' me bag. I need to see Cathy.'

Neither Billy nor Bernie would argue with her decision; knowing that if anyone could get through to Catherine, it would be Colleen and later that day she boarded *The Lucky Shamrock* to sail across the Irish Sea and be with Catherine.

LIVERPOOL 1893

Chapter 62

Broken Hearts

Billy and Colleen reached Great Newton Street a day later, after a rough, January crossing. John's kitchen was crowded, but there was nothing light-hearted about the gathering.

'Colleen! What are you doin' here?' Paddy asked, surprised at his daughter's appearance. 'What's happen'n on the farm?'

'Da! It's good to see you,' Colleen exclaimed, running to her father's arms. It was evident that Paddy wasn't too interested in the farm at that moment. There was a brief murmur of joy around the room, as people registered the fact that Colleen had arrived from Ireland, but silence soon resumed.

'Where's Catherine?' Billy asked, afraid that something dreadful had happened in his absence.

'She's in her bed, Bill,' Alfie answered, quietly. 'She took a bad turn last night; Daddy found her at the bottom of the stairs when he got home. Reckon she fainted an' fell from the top. We got the doctor in. It doesn't look good. He said it's consumption, and that she hasn't the will to fight it. The shock of Tom's death was too much for her an' she was weak already. The doctor said she hit her head in the fall as well, he said she has a fight ahead and if she doesn't pick up it'll be the broken heart that kills her, because it's stopping her from trying.' These words he whispered in his brother's ear, and their eyes met in deep sorrow at the thought of losing their beloved big sister. 'Maude and Daddy are with her...'

Coleen glanced around the silent room; Sarah and heavily pregnant Ethel were seated at the table, eyes red rimmed with crying. Mrs. Brown, the dress-maker was serving tea and sandwiches, and Sadie, after hearing about Catherine's condition, had brought oven fresh buns and was busy arranging them on the best china. Dennis and Elizabeth sat together in a corner of the room, and the clock on the mantle ticked.

'Let's go up there,' Colleen whispered to the boys. 'Sure, she'll want us with her.' The three made their way up the narrow staircase to Catherine's bedroom, barely able to speak. Would their Cathy leave them in this world to live on without her? Surely not.

'Colleen, come on in, and the boys! Cathy, look who's here to see you.' Maude feigned cheer. 'All the way from Ireland, our very own Colleen! Come and sit here beside Cathy. She'd love you to hold her hand and tell her a bit about the farm, I'm sure.'

Catherine stirred beneath the blankets; she turned her face towards Colleen, who strove to hide her horror when she saw the translucent, white pallor of the lovely face she knew so well. 'Sure Cathy darl'n. I'm after just leavin' the farm an' crossin' the stormy sea to see you, so I am. An' look at you so sick an' all,' she managed to say, while thoughts of Catherine's impending death filled her mind.

'Where's Bernie?' Catherine asked.

'She's on the farm Cathy. Sent me to see how y'are and ask if you'd want to come over when your better?' Colleen replied, attempting to offer her friend a reason to live. 'Sure we'll have a great time. Did Billy tell you I have a horse? I called him Clancy because he's always stitchin' me up an' throwin' me off so he is.' Colleen was fighting the tears and Billy came to her aid.

'We'll make the trip to Bray when you come over. It's the sea-side, but you'll have to be stronger sis.'

Catherine's pale blue eyes were clouding and the lamp flickered, casting shadows on the walls of her little room. She looked at each of them in turn and smiled, serenely peaceful.

'I have to go,' she said, her voice soft and clear. 'It won't be so bad for me. I'll be with Mammy and Tom, and I don't want you to be sad. I love you all so much. Dear Alfie, please work hard at Dooley's and make me and Mammy proud. Sarah is the girl for you. Look after her. Billy, have a great life on the waves. I'm so proud of my brothers. Maude and Colleen my angels, my heroes, be happy always. Go to Ireland and think of me. I'll be with you. Daddy,' she turned to John who clung to her hand intent on keeping her in this world. 'This time you stayed, Daddy. Mammy will be pleased about that and I'm sure she'll forgive you.'

The room fell silent. John, Billy, Alfie, Maude and Colleen were motionless until Catherine drifted quietly into an everlasting sleep, and then they stayed in mournful vigil until Sarah tapped gently on the door and, realising that Catherine had passed away, she took Alfie's hand and led him out.

BRAY, IRELAND 1896

Chapter 63

A glistening Irish Sea lapped the shoreline at Bray, churning sea bleached shingles, and a warm breeze brought gusts of salty air across the water, carrying with it the aroma of ocean; seagulls soared overhead, flashes of pure white against a clear blue sky. Alfie and Sarah strolled hand in hand, Billy and Colleen splashed, barefoot, in and out of the waves, Bernie and Seamus, now husband and wife, cooed over their new-born baby, Fionuala, Maude raced her siblings along the seashore, Elizabeth and Dennis marvelled at the distant horizon; accustomed to the confines of city life, the huge expanse of sky and sea acted as a healing balm to their troubled souls and, trailing behind a little came John and Sadie, now planning a life together and Paddy and Ethel, now settled on the farm, with their toddler daughter, Catherine, holding hands between them and thoroughly enjoying the sights and sounds of the seaside

Their long planned gathering, in memory of Catherine, had finally come about.

THE END

Printed in Great Britain
by Amazon

29848481R00098